Destination Liberation

Destination Liberation

M.A. Maya

ALLIED PUBLISHERS PVT. LTD.

Noida • Mumbai • Kolkata • Chennai • Bangalore

ALLIED PUBLISHERS PRIVATE LIMITED

D-5, Sector-2, **Noida**–201 301
Ph. Nos.: 0120-4320295/2542557/4352866
E-mail: delhi.books@alliedpublishers.com

17 Chittaranjan Avenue, **Kolkata**–700072
Ph.: 033-22129618 • E-mail: cal.books@alliedpublishers.com

15 J.N. Heredia Marg, Ballard Estate, **Mumbai**–400001
Ph.: 022-42126969 • E-mail: mumbai.books@alliedpublishers.com

No. 25/10, Commander-in-Chief Road, Ethiraj Lane (Next to Post Office)
Egmore, **Chennai**–600008
Ph.: 044-28223938 • E-mail: chennai.books@alliedpublishers.com

P.B. No. 9932, No. 15, 3rd Floor (Next to Vijaya Bank), 5th Cross, Gandhinagar,
Karnataka, **Bangalore**–560009. Ph.: 080-41530285 / 22386239
E-mail: bngl.journals@alliedpublishers.com / apsabng@airtelmail.in

Website: www.alliedpublishers.com

ISBN: 978-93-90951-87-1

Published by Sunil Sachdev and printed by Ravi Sachdev
at Allied Publishers Pvt. Ltd., D-5, Sector-2, Noida–201 301

To my childhood friends,

Jayanti Rajan and Jaishankar Singallur

Life is partly what we make it, and partly what it is made by the friends we choose.

—*Tennessee Williams*

Foreword

I know you are tired but come, this is the way.

—Rumi

The ultimate goal of every religion is to attain liberation from death and suffering. Spiritual Liberation has many names such as, Moksha, Salvation, Nirvana, Mukti, and Enlightenment. After a brief introduction to meditation, in a course conducted by the Art of Living foundation, Tara sets out on a journey to understand God and achieve Nirvana.

Following the footsteps of spiritual leaders, Tara travels extensively across India, chasing river sources and holy places. Her childhood friend Jaya accompanies her, from time to time, on this quest. They go to Varanasi and also go for the Chardham yatra in the Himalayas, all the while chasing Moksha and the River Ganga.

In her travels, Tara gets to learn about the political, religious, and cultural history of India. She reaches difficult destinations with the help of exceptionally kind guides. Tara gains a deep sense of pride in India as a country. She also loses her baggage of disappointments and expectations and becomes relatively calm and peaceful. However, it is said by holy men on Indian streets, that if you ever find God, it will be within yourself.

Back home, Tara practices Vipassana meditation, regularly. She also starts reading the Bhagavad Gita, under the guidance, of her friend Jai. After an intense process of letting go of everything she learned in her lifetime, Tara arrives at convincing answers about God and Moksha.

M.A. Maya

Contents

CHAPTER 1

God

Tara was sitting in church, as usual, at the stairs in front of the altar, with other children. This is where all the children gathered and sat during Sunday mass. No one paid any attention to the priest. They learned new games and heard new stories. Once in a while, some grown up person would hush them up. But soon the chatter would continue like a soft humming. Tara had made a friend, who, she would seek out every Sunday to sit with.

"Did you buy your new dress for Christmas?" asked Tara's friend.

"New dress? No" said Tara.

"You are supposed to buy new clothes for Christmas" said Tara's friend.

Tara was about three years old and had no idea that she had to buy new clothes for Christmas. She was really embarrassed that she had missed this important duty.

"Are we supposed to buy new clothes for Christmas?" Tara asked her mother on the way home from church.

"Oh yes! Everyone buys new clothes for Christmas" said Tara's mother. If Tara's mother had intended to not buy new clothes before, now it was out of question. Tara's mother was busy the next week procuring new clothes for the family.

"I am getting new clothes for Christmas too" said Tara to her friend the next Sunday. Her friend nodded and all was well in their world.

Years passed without anything happening and one day Tara was going to Sunday school. This was to prepare her, for her first holy communion. Every Sunday, Tara learned about honesty, kindness, and other virtues. Finally, the day of the Holy Communion arrived. But before she could receive communion, she had to confess.

"What should I tell the priest?" asked Tara.

"All your sins" said her aunt.

"Like what?" asked Tara. Tara was less than ten years old and she had not sinned much.

"Like if you told lies" said her aunt.

"I never told lies" said Tara. Tara could not remember any lies.

"You disobeyed your parents" continued her aunt.

"Yes, that I did often" said Tara, happy, that she had some sins in her bag.

"I wish I had a bigger list of sins" said Tara woefully.

"You lost your temper. You did not share your sweets. You can say all this" said Tara's aunt.

"Okay" said Tara feeling confident.

When Tara went to confess she added that she told lies. After all, a few sins are necessary to make an impression at her very first confession.

At Sunday school, Tara read about saints and how they saw God. Tara wanted to be a good Christian. She wanted to see God too. Every time she went to church, she concentrated hard on the statues trying to see God. After a while, she could see a smiling old man, with a long white beard, appear from one of the statues in church. But Tara knew very well it was her imagination. Though, she could make this old man appear time and again, she knew it was not God. She probably had to kneel for hours in snow like some saints or go to church every day before she saw God. Tara had limited time to seek God. She only went to church on Sundays. Every Sunday, Tara tried to see God. If she could manage to see God some Sunday, she would be happy. If not it was not meant to be.

One day Tara's dog died. Tara was heart broken. Tara wanted to see her dog again.

"Will I see my dog in heaven?" asked Tara to the church priest.

"Dogs do not go to heaven. Heaven is only for people" said the priest.

"There are no dogs in heaven?" asked Tara, really surprised.

"No. Only people" said the priest.

Tara immediately decided that she was not interested in going to heaven. Heaven would be boring if it had only people. And she started thinking about hell. People burning in an eternal fire did not make any sense. How can anyone burn so long? Later, in college years, the idea of heaven and hell was ridiculed in the books Tara read. There were so many theories about heaven and hell. Tara's favorite definition of hell was by Sartre - Hell is other people.

Though heaven, hell, and even God was confusing for Tara, she prayed regularly. She thanked God for everything. It was mostly out of habit. Over time, Tara stopped thinking about religion. She grew even skeptical about God. But she had read the bible a few times. Quoting the bible always helped her in her arguments with parents. If something was in the bible, it was right.

But once in a while, Tara would wonder about God. Whenever, Tara prayed, especially for someone else, her prayers were granted. It was with such regularity, that Tara was forced to think about some powerful force that had the power to grant boons and fix problems. Was there a God? Will Tara ever see God? Or was everything only coincidence?

CHAPTER 2

Art of Living

Tara was now in her forties. Her husband, Arjun, asked her to join an Art of living meditation course. Meditation courses had gained popularity among the Indian intellect. Meditation was helping people deal with work and culture stress. They recommended these courses to each other. Tara was cynical. Tara knew how to live life. Her life was full of accomplishments. Tara enjoyed every moment of her life and had a long list of fun things to do. Who could teach her the art of living? But Arjun insisted and Tara ended up showing up for the course.

The teacher was talking about how the course would help deal with self created problems.

"I do not create problems for myself. Others typically do that" protested Tara.

"If you go out for a walk and get dirty. What do you do? You come back home and shower. We will teach you how to take a spiritual bath that will get rid of problems created either by you or others" said the teacher.

Tara loved the reply and was hooked. It was Tara's first introduction to meditation. During meditation sessions, tears would flow down Tara's cheeks. How did she manage to gather so much stress in life? Life had taken her far away from herself. A lot of forgotten memories flooded her mind.

A different perspective of events began to unravel. She could see herself hurting others. Life was lived in such a rush. She did not take time out to see the effect of her words or actions on herself or others. All along, Tara thought she was perfect. She did no wrong. Meditation brought to light a different side of Tara.

And then the big event of the course happened. It was the evening for Sudarshan Kriya, which was a special kind of meditation invented by the Art of living Guru, Sri Sri Ravishankar. Tara had an out of body experience. She felt as though she was floating in the air. Then, she saw a bright light and Jesus hugging her and saying "I will always be there for you." Tara could not understand what happened to her. She was embarrassed to discuss her experience. She was dazed. When Tara, finally, told her friend, Jaya, about her experience, Jaya explained that her chakras might have opened up. Jaya, then went on to describe the seven chakras, which were energy points, in a human body. And thus, began Tara's journey to understand what it was that she experienced. This was not her imagination. She had not willed this experience. Meditation was reconnecting Tara to her younger innocent self. Sudarshan Kriya took her back to the time she really believed in Jesus. Tara was back to her childhood search of finding God.

Tara was eternally grateful she took the Art of living course. She never thought such popular programs would be of any value. She realized that foundations like the Art of living was doing a great service to humanity by introducing common people to meditation. Everyone who took the course gained something from it. For Tara, it opened up a whole new pursuit. "If you ever experience God, it will be within you," Tara had heard wise men say. Tara knew she had found a great tool in meditation. Meditation seemed to make her grow spiritually. It calmed her. She looked visibly more peaceful than before. Meditation brought a new urgency to understand the divine.

Life had brought Tara back to India, which she considered the greatest place on earth to explore spirituality. Tara had read many inspiring quotes about India. She read that Martin Luther King Jr. once stated "To other countries, I may go as a tourist, but to India, I come as a pilgrim." Mark Twain had once said that "Nothing has been left undone, either by man or nature, to make India the most extraordinary country that the Sun visits on his round. Nothing seems to have been forgotten, nothing overlooked." He also said that "India has two million gods, and worships them all. In religion all other countries are paupers. India is the only millionaire."

Tara was thrilled to be in India, the country where she was born. She had been away from India for more than two decades. Tara's friend Jaya was a Hindu by birth. Tara sought Jaya's help in understanding Hinduism. Together, they decided to explore India's spirituality.

CHAPTER 3

Varanasi

Spiritual journeys involve travel. Indians know this. It begins with moving physically to new places, and then slowly transcending ideas and beliefs. The first place Tara and Jaya decided to visit was Varanasi which was also known as Kashi. This is considered one of the holiest places in Hinduism. The two women did not know what to expect. They prepared for the journey so that they may be ready to accept whatever blessings came their way. Tara meditated regularly. She collected plenty of information about Varanasi from the internet and books. Jaya also intensified her prayer rituals. The families of Jaya and Tara were afraid that they might leave home for good and become sadhus. No one knew what would happen.

It was a long trip to Varanasi. Two pampered women, with a lot of luggage, set out for Varanasi. After a long flight, they reached Varanasi. The roads were narrow and the hotel they were staying in, was not accessible to cars. Thus, they walked a couple of miles dragging their suitcases towards their residence. It was a sunny morning on a Sunday. The cooks were on leave. Thus, when they reached the hotel, they had to make do with some cold bread and tea for breakfast. It was not a great start. The best was yet to come. The ghats were just behind the hotel. Thus, the ghats were easily accessible to them. After breakfast, Tara and Jaya rushed to the ghats and they saw the river Ganga for the first time. They had read so much about the Ganges. And now they were seeing it. They touched the water and paid respects to the river, before taking a long walk on the ghats. They were very happy. They sat on the steps of the ghats and drank some warm ginger tea. Stray dogs and cows roamed everywhere. Varanasi was kind. They welcomed all living beings. The two women were warned to be careful of cheats. However, they felt no fear. It was as though they owned the city and they had walked on these ghats all their lives. Moreover, the meals at the hotel also became delicious. Hot, fresh, vegetarian, and sattvic meals. It was just the start that seemed difficult. Varanasi, soon, became home.

A dip in Ganga is believed to wash away all the sins of a lifetime. The Ganges was known as the most polluted river on earth. Many people advised the two women against taking a dip. But Jaya and Tara were determined to take a Ganga snan. The hotel staff said that the best time for a Ganga snan was at four in the morning. Tara and Jaya woke up early in the morning and arrived at the Ghats sharply at four. The boatman, they had arranged in advance, decided to take foreigners with him. Jaya was angry.

"Wait, another boatman is coming" said the boatman.

"Not fair to make us wait" said Jaya.

But soon a wise old boatman arrived. He took Tara and Jaya to a place with plenty of privacy and tents for changing. He waited at a respectful distance as the two women engaged in their bath ritual. The waters were ice cold. But Tara had never felt this great. She felt charged. Jaya was really happy and chanted prayers loudly. Jaya prayed for everyone. Family, friends, world. She prayed for Tara to get a Noble prize.

Tara was amused and touched. Jaya had a large heart. Jaya was clearly grateful to do her Ganga snan and she remained on a high the rest of the day.

The boatman took them back to the shore. The ladies gave him a big tip. He was very touched with the big tip.

"You deserve the money. You made Ganga snan possible for us" said Jaya.

Later Jaya said that she was glad she got this boatman. A wise old boatman, somehow, was more appropriate than the young guy they had chosen the previous day. On the way back they rescued a drowning owl. People had spotted the owl and asked the boatman to rescue it. He picked the owl and placed it under a basket in the boat. In the evening, when the wings were dry, the owl would fly away. People of Varanasi were kind to all creatures.

Varanasi was a place where most people went to perform rituals for dead relatives. But many great spiritual leaders found their Gurus there. Tara had secretly hoped to find a Guru in Varanasi. One evening, after dinner, Tara decided to spend some time alone on the Ghats. Jaya was busy with some phone calls. Tara was enjoying the flow of the river and a gentle breeze. One young man approached her and started chatting with her.

"What is your purpose of visiting Kashi?" the boy asked. "Actually I wanted to find a Guru. They say there are many Mahatmas in Kashi. I did not spot any" said Tara.

"One Mahatma is visiting. I will take you to him" said the boy.

Tara followed him to a place where a sadhu was sitting. The Sadhu was smoking a chillum.

"I would love to get some gyan from you if possible" said Tara humbly.

"Where are you from?" asked the Sadhu.

"Mangalore" answered Tara.

"I have been to Mangalore. Everyone eats fish there" said the Sadhu.

"Yes. Lots of people love fish in Mangalore" agreed Tara. "First, you will eat the fish. Then the fish will become worms and eat you" said the Sadhu.

Tara was guilty of regularly eating fish. She waited for the Sadhu to say something else. But he went on and on about the fish eating habits of people from Mangalore. He clearly did not approve of eating fish. After some time Tara asked his leave. When she got back to the hotel, Tara could not stop laughing at the fish eating gyan she got. Jaya scolded her for talking to chillum smoking strangers. Perhaps, if she had stayed longer, Tara would find a Guru. But the women were there only for three days. Not enough time to find a Guru.

Tara and Jaya had no idea what was expected of them in Varanasi. They decided to follow their hearts.

"Wherever great people walk, they leave their energy. We must try and absorb that energy" said Jaya.

Almost every spiritual leader of India has walked on the Varanasi Ghats. Tara and Jaya always kept that in mind and they loved their walks on the Ghats. Every evening, they attended the Ganga Arti, which was prayers to the river Ganga. For thousands of years, every morning and evening, the Ganga arti was performed on these Ghats. The place was lit with lamps and the sounds of bhajans filled the air. It was timeless and magical. Tara and Jaya felt really blessed to witness the Ganga artis. They somehow wanted to take a bit of Varanasi back with them. They focused on the energies of the place. Sometimes, they did not feel anything. But, in

Sarnath, where Buddha gave his first sermon, the energies gave both of them goosebumps. Tara and Jaya, immediately, sat down, and breathed in deeply. They chanted Om three times. Was that Buddha's energy they witnessed? They hoped it would be. They were naive but their desire to reach God was strong.

When they visited temples Jaya would recite mantras and Tara would sit beside her and meditate or study the energies of the place. Thus, they always spend more time on temple premises compared to regular people. Most people, typically, left soon after Darshan. Tara had not interacted with temple priests before. Their roles were limited to artis and giving prasad. But here in Varanasi, priests would seek tourists out and perform special rituals for them. For a small fee, they would pray for her family, ancestors, her well-being in terms of wealth and health.

They wanted the world for her. They would tie a lot of strings on her wrists and apply fragrant pastes on her forehead. Also put flower garlands on her neck. If Tara's family thought she would abandon them in Varanasi, they were really wrong. The temple priests always made it a point to remind her of her family. "The priests are sweet talking you out of your money. They are shrewd. They play with your psychology." This was what some people had to say. But there were very few people in Tara's life who would want so much good for her. She loved the sweet talk. The fees was so small compared to what they were wishing for her. They wished more good for her than she would wish for herself. Temple priests always remained feel good people for Tara, after her trip to Varanasi.

CHAPTER 4

Mannikarnika Ghat

Varanasi was a place to eat and shop. The hotel provided excellent meals. Sometimes Jaya and Tara ate out. The back roads were tiny. But they contained shops that sold the best silk and cotton. Tara went on a shopping spree. No one would think she had any spiritual goals looking at how she was buying away. Jaya was trying to practice minimalism and restrained from buying. But even Jaya succumbed time and again to all the beautiful things Varanasi had to offer. They ate Banarasi paan and bought shell bangles.

"When the shell bangles break, assume that some bad luck has left you" explained the shopkeeper.

"Are these red bangles really lac? They look like plastic to me" said Tara.

"They are lac. Hundred percent" said the shopkeeper.

Tara was not sure. But she did not know how to test for lac. She decided to consider it lac. Both Jaya and Tara were happy to wear their bangles for the rest of the trip.

"We look like Bengalis" said Tara. Married Bengali women, typically, wore white shell and red lac bangles.

Manikarnika Ghat was the place where they burned dead bodies. At any given time, day or night, there were a couple of bodies burning at this Ghat. Tara and Jaya had seen the place a few times during their walks. If Tara saw a dead person, normally, the sight would linger in her mind for a few days. She would be disturbed. Strangely, in Varanasi, the burning dead bodies did not bother Tara or Jaya.

"I have rituals to do at a temple. It will take time. What do you want to do in the meanwhile?" asked Jaya.

"I will meditate" said Tara.

"Good. They say one must meditate by the Manikarnika Ghat. The pranas (life forces) leaving the dead people are energies conducive to meditation" said Jaya.

It was a thing to try and this was opportunity. After Jaya left for the temple, Tara found a spot from where she could see the Manikarnika ghat and the smoke emitting from the burning bodies. And suddenly, the intensity of what she was witnessing hit her. Every couple of minutes, a dead person arrived at the Ghat to be burned. This happened all day and night. Nowhere else in the world so many dead bodies arrive at a place. There was no war nor an epidemic. This was a glimpse of how the world dies on a normal day.

Suddenly, Tara was filled with a great sadness. She understood what death was for the first time. Everyone who was alive at that moment would die. This was a different kind of understanding of death. Perhaps the prana leaving the bodies imparted their sadness to Tara. Or perhaps the pranas conveyed something about death to Tara. But she knew that she understood death more than most people from now on. Ganga arti was going to start. Many old people with happy faces were dancing and singing. But they were all going to die.

Tears rolled down Tara's face. She cried and cried. She cried because everyone was going to die. Jaya was at a loss when she came back and saw Tara crying because everyone was going to die. Everyone knew this. But Jaya understood somehow that Tara needed to cry this out. She did not say anything and just sat beside her. They both watched the Ganga arti and Tara sobbed the whole time.

When the arti ended, Tara sobered up. Every evening, people who regularly witnessed the burning of dead bodies, gathered on the ghats to do arti to the river. They were not crying. They were singing and dancing. They were celebrating life. Perhaps they understood death as well as Tara did. Perhaps they did not. It did not matter. Tara looked at them and decided she would not cry for death any more.

It was time to leave Varanasi. Jaya got a lunch of puris and stuffed chili pickles packed for lunch. They had lunch at the airport. The hotel staff had packed them way too many puris. They thought they would share it with others. There were many foreigners at the airport.

"Ask that guy if he wants some lunch. He has been looking at us for some time" said Jaya.

"Would you like to have some puris" asked Tara.

"No. But I was wondering how you were eating the chilies" said the foreigner.

"Try some" said Tara.

"No thanks" said the foreigner.

It was a common trick to make foreigners eat chilies and see them react. But this was not the right place or time for such tricks. Tara decided to give away the lunch to airport staff, instead. They would fly to Mumbai and meet school friends. Tara and Jaya looked forward to meeting everyone.

CHAPTER 5

Shirdi

By the time Tara got to Mumbai, she caught laryngitis and lost her voice. Ravi, who was their classmate, picked them up from airport and took Tara directly to a doctor. Ravi's wife Sabia made her kada which was a drink with plenty of herbs. She also gave Tara steam inhalation. Tara was feeling a lot better.

"Next time I come, I am going to make sure I get laryngitis. So that I can get some attention too" said Jaya. Everyone laughed. Sabia was very loving. She paid prompt attention to Jaya.

The next day they went to Sanju's house. Sanju was also their classmate. Sanju had a big spread for breakfast. Sabia had already fed Jaya and Tara a lot. Clearly, good food was everywhere. A dozen friends had already gathered at Sanju's house. And they all proceeded to Shirdi.

"I love Shirdi. I can take you there a hundred times" said Sanju to the group. Sanju did not visit temples too often, but he was always game for Shirdi. This was Tara's first trip to Shirdi. Tara was happy she was traveling with school friends. This trip was not like Varanasi. In Varanasi, Tara and Jaya were alert and making all the plans. Here, they sat back and relaxed. They were taken care of. It felt good. Tara felt like she was in high school again. Years of living apart did not matter in this trip.

They stopped at Reena's hotel in Nashik, for the night. Reena was Sanju's sister who was also their classmate. Reena's hotel was grand and she offered them tea with cakes, pastries, and many other dishes. Tara and her friends were bombarded with good food. Life was good. The plan for the evening was to chill and talk. They were all meeting after decades. There was so much catching up to do. Tara was happy all her friends were doing well. They had all turned out to be good human beings desiring happiness for others. A little like the Varanasi priests.

"Let's go to Trimbakeshwar temple. It is very close from here" said Jaya.

"We were planning to party, no?" asked Tara.

"Let us just chill" said Sanju.

"Jai has been telling me about this temple. I want to go" said Jaya.

"It has one of the twelve jyothirlingas. You already saw one jyothirlinga in Kashi Vishwanath temple at Varanasi. This is another. Moreover, the source of the Godavari river is in this temple" said Jai.

Soon, everyone decided to go to the temple. It was a grand old stone temple. After darshan, Jaya sat down on the floor, and sang bhajans. A few other people in the group also joined her. Jaya soon had a meltdown. She was weeping. Another friend Durga also had a similar experience. Meltdowns are part of spiritual progress. This was a process of letting go and feeling lighter in spirit and mind. Tara had her meltdown at Varanasi, Jaya had hers at Trimbakeshwar. What triggers these meltdowns are hard to explain. Meltdowns, seeing bright lights, and other such experiences act like rewards and encourage the seeker to keep going.

Reena joined them on their trip to Shirdi. Reena did not expect to enjoy the company of school friends so much. She had, initially, limited her role to playing host at Nashik. But she stayed talking late in to night and also came on the journey to Shirdi. Reena was a rich and busy woman. Her circle of friends, now, were big shots in society. But something about childhood friendships was healing and comforting. Everyone had come a long way from high school. They had mostly done well. But there were unfinished dreams and unexpected challenges. Life was not easy. They talked to each other about their problems and dreams. It was easy to open up. They knew they were safe. These people they had known forever. Tara wanted to help everyone. She could not. She decided that wishing them well was all she could do. Perhaps that was all that was necessary. To each their own journey.

Religious places always emitted a calming energy. But sometimes, Tara would feel a whiff of powerful energy. At Shirdi, she felt that when they were standing in the long queue for Darshan. Though Reena had got them VIP passes, the last part of the queue was unavoidable. There was a lot of rushing and pushing. The devotees were chanting loudly. Amongst all the chaos, Tara felt an intense energy that gave her goosebumps. She knew this energy was created by the throngs of devotees visiting Shirdi every day. The faith of the devotees was what made Shirdi such a spiritual center. The more intense the faith, the more spiritual the place becomes.

After darshan, Jaya and a few others, sat on the temple floor and sang bhajans. Suddenly a dog appeared and placed his head on Liz's lap. Liz had spend her lifetime giving out love. She was a widow and had many responsibilities. Liz always remained optimistic, cheerful, and jocular. It was no surprise that the dog sought her out from the crowd. Everyone in the temple was really surprised. The dog made himself very comfortable and slept. The bhajan singing was like lullaby to him.

"Must be Saibaba. He is pleased with your singing" said someone.

"Bhairava" called out Jaya to the dog. Some people in the crowd passed on biscuits. Jaya gave it to the dog. The dog ate happily.

Soon, it was lunch time. Tara wanted to eat langar which was meals offered by the temple at Shirdi.

"Let us get some good food. Some chicken and stuff" said Sanju.

Tara was a little disappointed. She really wanted to eat langar. She had read a lot about it. The temple offered food to devotees because Saibaba also used to cook meals and feed visitors. The temple kitchen was progressive and used solar energy. The number of people who partook of meals in Shirdi was staggering. But there was always enough for all. Tara had watched many documentaries about Shirdi langar.

"If you really want to eat langar, you must ask. We will work towards making it happen" said Reena.

Insisting on something was not a habit of Tara. She was happy that Reena understood that she really wanted to eat langar. Sanju was a little disappointed but everyone ignored him. Reena arranged meal tickets for all. The langar was one of the most delicious meals Tara ate in her life. It was a simple vegetarian meal and was very satisfying. Everyone including Sanju was happy with the lunch.

The trip ended with dinner at Sanju's house. Sanju made Makkai ki roti and sarson ka saag for dinner. That was a perfect meal after a long journey. It was delicious and memorable. After that, Tara and her friends would request the same dishes, every time, they visited Sanju's house. Makkai ki roti and sarson ka saag became signature Sanju's household meal after that trip.

The Mumbai trip did Tara and Jaya as much good as the Varanasi trip. Both the trips were equally healing. They decided to go to the Himalayas in two years time. They invited all their classmates to join them on the trip. Tara and Jaya decided to prepare their minds and bodies for the great Himalayan journey. They would meet again only after two years.

CHAPTER 6

Vipassana

After Varanasi, Tara wanted to intensify her spiritual practices. Her husband, Arjun, was a Vipassana practitioner. Vipassana was a meditation technique taught by Buddha himself. In India, Vipassana courses taught by S.N. Goenka was a minimum of ten days. You were not allowed to speak for ten days. This was considered a tough course. There were many centers to take the course. Tara decided to go to Kerala to take her first Vipassana course. If Vipassana course did nothing for her, there would be no loss. Kerala was beautiful and it was her ancestral place. Tara loved visiting Kerala.

Arjun dropped her at the Mangalore train station at five in the morning. She caught the Parashuram express to Chengannur. Parashuram Express had a pantry. From the beginning of the trip banana pori, chili bhajjis, parippu vadas, and many other delicious snacks were offered on the train. Tara was seated in an air conditioned compartment and she ate and ate. She was having a great time. This was one of the best train trips she ever took. At Chengannur, there was a flight of stairs to climb down and Tara struggled with her large suitcase. Tara did not know how to travel light. She hired a rickshaw to the Vipassana center.

Tara was amongst the last to arrive. A small crowd of meditators had already arrived at the center. They were drinking tea and making friends. One organizer showed Tara to the place where tea was served. Some others helped her with her luggage. After meals, it was the rule, that, everyone had to wash their own plates and cups. After tea, Tara finished her registration for the course. She had to hand over her mobile phones, valuables, and wallet to keep in a secure locker. She will get all these back only at the end of the course.

The tea was the last meal of the day. There would be no dinner throughout the course. The meals served at the center were always excellent. Warm vegetarian Kerala meals of rice, sambhar, and vegetables. Puttukadala, idlis, appams, and dosas were served at breakfast. Sometimes banana leaves wrapped snacks were served at tea. All these were prepared fresh at the center by volunteers. There were no fees for taking the course. Only donations and volunteers ran the center. Tara was glad she chose to come to Kerala. At this center, nature presented itself in all its glory. There was greenery as far as eyes could see. Pleasant sounds of chirping birds were ever present. The place was serene.

They gathered at the meditation hall to get their first instructions of the course. The teacher S.N. Goenka was no more. His teachings were conveyed via video recordings. There was another teacher in the meditation hall to clarify doubts and maintain order. There were also assistant teachers who lived with the students at the dorms. Tara had seen many YouTube videos where people talked about their experiences during Vipassana meditation. She was eager to see what her experience would be. She was expecting something magical to happen that would change her life. However, the first thing she was told was to suspend all her expectations, beliefs, and prejudices for the duration of the course which was ten days, and to go with the flow. Every day, Goenkaji would give them tasks. They were to only focus on those tasks. And from then on, no one should communicate with anyone else, both, verbally or non-verbally. In fact, they were advised to avoid eye contact. The only people they were allowed to talk to were their teachers. That too, only if talking was absolutely necessary. This course was about a journey within. There was no room for inputs from outside of any kind.

The meditations started at four thirty in the morning followed by breakfast at six thirty. Typically, they would go back to meditate in the meditation hall at eight. But on the first day they were allowed to meditate in their rooms. Everyone in Tara's dorm went to sleep. They woke up only at lunch which was served at eleven. Clearly, it was not a good idea to meditate in the rooms. Tara diligently spend all her time in the meditation hall from then on. Thus, Tara was there from four thirty in the morning to nine in the night, with a couple of hours of breaks in between for rest, meals, and wash.

The meditations started with watching your breath and then slowly scanning your entire body for sensations. Goenkaji was, repeatedly, throughout the course, asking everyone to observe the sensations with equanimity. Sensations were memories of experiences stored in your body. The reactions to these sensations generate deep rooted habit patterns called sankaras. Sankaras are the root cause of misery. For example, if a dog bit you when you were a child, your reaction to a dog is aversion. The habit pattern of fearing a dog needs to be eradicated to become at ease with a dog. The other thing he stressed on was to observe annica which was the constant change happening within you. Any sensation that arose would soon pass away. Nothing was permanent. Everything was annica.

As Tara sat in meditation for hours at a stretch, she experienced pains and aches in certain parts of her body, which she had not noticed before. The pains gradually disappeared to only bring about new aches and pain in different parts of her body. These painful sensations were called gross sensations by Goenkaji. Tara could also sense vibrations inside her which got intense as days went by. These were called subtle sensations. Tara's aim was to attain bhanga which is a state where your entire system collapses in to subtle vibrations. Tara was getting restless. Her aches and pains were not going away. Her teacher explained that her state was due to her cravings and aversions.

"Remain equanimous" said the teacher.

"I quickly scan through my gross sensations. Not paying attention to it at all" said Tara.

"Ignore all sensations. All reactions are bad. They create new sankaras" said the teacher.

"Oh, I must ignore the subtle sensations too?" asked Tara.

"Yes, remain equanimous" said the teacher.

Finally, Tara understood what equanimity was. There were only a couple of days left for the course to end. Tara learned to not react to any sensations as she scanned her body. And she experienced bhanga for the first time. Free flow of vibrations throughout her body. Tara felt happy and at peace. But even bhanga was annicca. This state would change too. Anything that arises passes away soon.

"Anicca, Anicca, Anicca" Tara could hear Goenkaji repeat. According to Vipassana teachings, there are only two reactions to the sensations—craving or aversion. If you liked the sensation you begin to crave for it, if you did not, you begin to hate it. Both reactions create sankaras. Vipassana teaches you to not react to sensations, that is to remain equanimous.

Equanimity is the greatest virtue for a Vipassana meditator. By not reacting to the sensations, Tara was changing lifelong habit patterns, that is destroying sankaras. In ten days, Tara had scanned a lot of memories, in the form of sensations, whose contents she did not remember. Some memories were supposed to be from previous births. But she had altered the way she reacted to them forever. In Goenkaji's words, she had performed surgery at a molecular level.

Vipassana meditation made Tara realize, for the first time, that memories were not stored only in the brain, but all over the body. It also made her think about the constant vibrations within her body. Goenkaji had mentioned that there was no solidity in the universe. There was only vibrations. In fact, there was a branch of science that said the entire universe was made of strings of energy. The strategy of Tara and Jaya observing energies of certain places made even more sense to her now.

When Tara got back home, she stayed in a state of ecstasy for a couple of days. She had big plans. The bhanga she experienced in Kerala made her affectionate towards the universe. She had found a great tool in Vipassana meditation which would help her find the truth. But soon, she found Vipassana meditation difficult to practice. It would take a couple more ten day meditation courses before she could do Vipassana meditation on her own. For now, she returned to guided meditations by the Guru of the Art of living foundation, Sri Sri Ravishankar. There was still time for the Himalayan trip. Tara searched for new ways to upgrade her spiritual state. More pilgrimages seemed to be the way forward.

CHAPTER 7

Kanyakumari

After her train trip to Kerala, Tara looked forward to more train trips. Kanyakumari was in her bucket list to visit. Three oceans, namely, the Arabian sea, the Indian ocean, and the Bay of Bengal met at Triveni Sangam in Kanyakumari. To see sunrise and sunset at the confluence of the three oceans was Tara's long time desire. Moreover, she would take her favorite train Parashuram express to travel to Kanyakumari. Arjun decided to travel along with Tara to Kanyakumari. They got down at Thiruvananthapuram station and traveled by car to Kanyakumari. Thiruvananthapuram was in Kerala. So they would be seeing a little of Kerala too. Tara loved to visit Kerala. She could feel the loving presence of her ancestors in Kerala. Every bit of Kerala was home.

Their first stop was at Arapally in Thiruvithamcode which was a church believed to be constructed by Saint Thomas. Saint Thomas was one of the twelve apostles of Jesus Christ. Tara belonged to the Syro Malabar community of Kerala who claimed that they were among the first Christians of the world and were converted by Saint Thomas himself. Tara had her own doubts about this claim. Tara had not seen any validation of this claim from the Catholic church in Rome. The main cause of Christianity in India, in general, was the arrival of European missionaries. In this trip, Tara learned for the first time about the eight churches build by

St. Thomas in Kerala. They were called Seven and a half churches because of Arapally. Arapally meant half church in Malayalam. No one exactly knew why it was called half church. Arapally was constructed out of black stone like old Hindu temples. It definitely was ancient. Tara would have loved to see some Carbon dating validation. She set her doubts aside and looked around. There were oil lamps everywhere. There was a wooden Cross said to have been placed by St. Thomas, himself, in 63 AD. The architecture of the church was definitely Indian. Unlike new churches build by missionaries, there was no European art or influence. This church was definitely different. It was supposed to be the oldest functioning church in the world. After the Arapally visit, Tara was more curious than ever about the history of the Syro Malabar church.

Swami Vivekananda was an Indian philosopher who was well known for his speech to the 1893 Parliament of Religions in Chicago, where he introduced Hinduism to America. The Vivekanadapuram Ashram in Kanyakumari was based on the teachings of Swami Vivekananda. Tara had booked for two people at the Vivekanadapuram Ashram but it was interpreted as two rooms.

So Arjun and Tara got independent rooms. The rooms were only two hundred rupees a night. They were clean and comfortable. There was a canteen that offered vegetarian meals at affordable prices. The campus was huge and beautiful.

That evening, Tara took her dip at Triveni sangam. She watched the sunset and the moon rise, both happening at the same time, immersed at the confluence of the three oceans. These waters had traveled far and will travel far. It carried so many memories and secrets. The first evening at

Kanyakumari was ethereal. There was a huge crowd at the seashore watching the sunset. The next two mornings, Tara went to Triveni Sangam, religiously, to the see the sun rise. But the Sun remained behind clouds. Tara had to return without seeing a Kanyakumari sunrise.

Tara also visited the Vivekananda rock memorial in Kanyakumari. Swami Vivekananda swam to this rock in the middle of the sea and meditated for three days and nights. He is said to have attained enlightenment on this rock. Tara wondered what enlightenment meant. She wanted to be enlightened too. The walls of the Vivekanadapuram Ashram were inscribed with Vivekananda quotes. Some of her favorite quotes were

"You cannot believe in God until you believe in yourself", "Where can we go to find God if we cannot see him in our own hearts and in every living being?", and

"As different streams having different sources all mingle their waters in the sea, so different tendencies, various though they appear, crooked or straight, all lead to God."

Tara found Vivekananda fascinating. She had learned about the life of Vivekananda as part of her school syllabus. But only in Vivekandapuram, she learned his teachings. She found his teaching universal and not confined to any religion.

Tara also visited the Gandhi Mandapam in Kanyakumari. Here Gandhi's ashes was kept in display before scattering it at the Triveni Sangam. Tara thought how apt it was for Gandhi to be dispersed where the three oceans met. Gandhi would travel far even after death.

On the way back, the car driver suggested a visit to Suchindram Temple. Suchindaram temple was not in the list of stops Tara had planned.

"There may not be enough time" said Tara.

"It is on the way. You must not miss this temple" insisted the driver.

Thus, they visited the Suchindaram temple. It was a beautiful, old, stone, temple with impressive sculptures. The temple had long corridors whose purpose was not clear. But suddenly, as Tara was walking along a corridor, she felt a whiff of powerful energy. For Tara, this energy meant that the place was super holy. Why this corridor was more holy for her instead of all the other religious places she visited in this trip, Tara could not tell. After her Vipassana experience, Tara knew that the vibrations of the place was affecting her own. It felt like a message. She lingered on the corridor for some time. When Tara returned to the car, she thanked the driver for the temple visit. It became one of the most poignant experiences in the entire trip.

Tara loved visiting palaces and imagine how people lived in it. All the palaces Tara visited so far, were made of marble or stone and covered with precious stones. Tara was eager to know how Kerala royalty lived in the past. Tara visited the Padmanabhapuram palace and the Kuthira mallika palace on the way back to the railway station. These palaces belonged to the past rulers of Travancore. Unlike other palaces Tara had seen, these palaces were mainly comfortable living. It was not gaudy or ostentatious. The Travancore royalty own immense wealth, even today. It is said that the royal treasure of gold and precious stones, safeguarded in the Padmanabhapuram palace temple, can fund entire nations. However, they did not show any desire to flaunt their wealth. Tara was impressed with their elegance and simplicity. These were talented and just rulers. One of the kings invented the dance form, Kathakali. They defeated the Dutch and Tippu

Sultan who came to conquer them. Tara understood that the main reason a small kingdom can defeat a huge power was good ethics. She was filled with a sense of pride about the history of her ancestral state of Kerala.

Back home, Tara displayed the seashells she got from the Kanyakumari beach. She burned the candles she bought from Arrappally. The glow of the trip stayed long with her. Tara had gone to Kanyakumari chasing the sunrise. She did not see any. Instead, she saw history. We seek something but we find something else. Nothing is wasted in travel.

CHAPTER 8

Madurai and Rameshwaram

After Kanyakumari, Tara and Arjun decided to take more train trips. They decided to visit the Jyothirlinga in Rameshwaram. There were a total of twelve Jyothirlingas and Tara had already seen the Jyothirlingas of Varanasi and Nashik. It was believed that visiting a Jyothirlinga would grant you moksha. India was divided in to states that were vastly different from each other in language, food, and fashion. Religion connected them. The Jyothirlingas were situated in different corners of India. If someone traveled from North India to Rameshwaram, he could not understand a single word of what the locals said. Yet, culture encouraged them to travel promising them even moksha which was the highest goal of every Hindu.

Enroute to Rameshwaram, Tara and Arjun took the train to Madurai and stayed at the T.M. Lodge. Madurai was famous for the Meenakshi amman temple. This lodge cost only a couple of hundred rupees for the night but was clean and tidy. The lodge was centrally located and really close to the Meenakshi amman temple. Everything about Madurai was heavenly. Excellent food everywhere. Good coffee, idlis, dosas, and chutneys. On the streets, they sold sundal which were delicious boiled pulses. The sweets of Madurai were out of this world. Tara gobbled on jehangiris and milk cakes. The fragrance of jasmine flowers permeated the entire city. Tara was really happy. She walked to the temple every morning and bought Sungudi sarees and jasmine oil. Madurai was all about excellent living.

After two nights in Madurai, Tara and Arjun took a train ride from Madurai to Rameshwaram. Rameshwaram was located on the island Pamban. The train ride included the Pamban bridge which connected Pamban to the mainland. The Pamban bridge was the first Indian sea bridge which covered more than two kilometers over the Bay of Bengal. It was one of the most pleasant train rides Tara took. Dozens of Peacocks flew all around the bridge. The sea water was crystal clean and they could see fish. Tara and Arjun sat on the floor of the train. It was one train trip Tara wanted to never end. It was like a dream.

At Rameshwaram, Tara and Arjun stayed at Hotel Tamilnadu. This hotel was very close to the temple. In the morning, Tara took a dip at Agneetheertham before going to the temple. Then, she took baths from twenty two holy wells at the temple. At each well, there was a priest who poured buckets of water on people. There were huge crowds at each well. Tara waited her turn patiently and made sure she was properly drenched with holy water. After that Tara went for darshan.

Tara and Arjun explored Rameshwaram by rickshaw. They also took a trip to Dhanushkodi by rickshaw. The entire ride was along the sea. On one side of the road was the Bay of Bengal and the other was the Indian ocean. At Dhanushkodi, the two oceans met. The roads, the water, and the air was very clean. This was divine. Not just temples and churches were holy. Tara was sure that nature was divine too.

Abdul Kalam who was a space scientist and later became the President of India, was born in Dhanushkodi. The place was sacred to Hindus because the Sethu bridge from Ramayana connected Dhanushkodi to Srilanka. This was also where India ended. About twenty kilometers away, across the ocean, was Srilanka. Dhanushkodi was abandoned after it was destroyed by a cyclone in 1964. Tara and Arjun roamed among the ruins of Dhanushkodi for a long time. After that, they ate a delicious lunch of fish and rice at a small roadside stall.

Later that day, they visited the house of Abdul Kalam in Rameshwaram. Nothing of Kalam was there. The house was filled with gift shops. Tara was disappointed at the state of his house. She had read Kalam's book "The wings of fire", at a stretch, without keeping it down. The book had really motivated her. Kalam was her childhood hero. The town had missed an opportunity of displaying the greatness of the man, Abdul Kalam, was.

When she got back home, Tara boiled all the flowers and herbs she got from the temples of Madurai and Rameshwaram in coconut oil. She had no heart to dispose of the many beautiful lotus flowers the temple priests gave her. This way, she got the best hair oil which kept her hair soft for days.

There were similarities in the trips to Kanyakumari and Rameshwaram. Both the places were confluences of oceans. The economies of both the places depended on seashells. In Kanyakumari, Tara traced the footsteps of Vivekananda. In Rameshwaram, she revisited Abdul Kalam. Both these men were important Indian historical figures. Also, Arjun accompanied her on these two trips.

"I am really getting to know India. I am bathing in her waters and engaging in her culture like never before" said Tara.

"You can become a politician now" said Arjun.

Politics was not on Tara's mind. She was getting ready to go to the Himalayas. She took the train to Kerala, again, for another ten day Vipassana course. Arjun came to drop her at the station. Arjun would soon leave for America. Their journeys were different from now on. It was raining and as the train left the station, Arjun's image blurred on the glass windows of her compartment. Tara was sad. After a few minutes, Jaya called to say she was traveling to Kerala too. She was visiting Sabarimala which was close to Chengannur where Tara was headed to. It was a wakeup call for Tara that the Himalayan trip was fast approaching. The parippu vadas and pazham poris also started to arrive. Tara was on her favorite train, Parashuram express, again. She pondered on what snacks to feast on first. Tara was back in the moment.

Tara could reach bhanga sooner in her second Vipassana course. At the end of each course, Tara felt a deep compassion for the universe. Vipassana Guru, Goenkaji, also talked a lot about compassion and goodwill for the universe. Every morning, during breakfast hour the song "Sab ka mangal ho", which meant let good things happen to all, would play in the center. Buddha had attained Nirvana. Nirvana meant becoming enlightened. No one could explain Nirvana to Tara. But she knew Nirvana was the ultimate goal of every spiritual seeker. Tara decided Nirvana would mean that she would personify compassion. She was only making guesses about Nirvana. Anyways, if she ever got there, she would know.

CHAPTER 9

Seven and a Half Churches

It so happened that a couple of churches from the list of the eight churches built by St. Thomas in India, were near the Chengannur Vipassana center. Tara decided to visit these churches, by car, before returning home. The first church she visited was the Nilackal church. It was situated close to the Sabarimala hills, in the middle of a dense jungle. Tara stopped at the foot of the Sabarimala hills for a while. At the top of those hills was the famous Sabarimala temple, that was forbidden for women below fifty. Jaya was there now. Tara had to wait a little longer before she could go. Tara had watched men getting ready for the Sabarimala temple from her childhood days. It was considered a dangerous journey through jungles filled with wild animals. So the men lead an austere life for a couple of months before the trip. Tara was thrilled to get here without much effort. May be she would come back some day to do darshan. But today she was heading to the Nilackal church.

The Nilackal church had shifted a couple of kilometers away from where St. Thomas had constructed the original church. A wooden cross, supposedly from the old church, was prominently displayed in the church. Wild elephants roamed in these parts. Religious retreats were held at the church from time to time. It was a beautiful place filled with nature. Tara loved the place and wished she could stay longer.

Her next stop was the Niranam church. It was a modern looking church except that the Pattamukkil family house was within the church compound. Traditionally, Hindu priests with their families lived within the temple premises. The Pattamukkil family was one of the four Hindu Brahmin families converted to Christianity by St. Thomas, in Niranam. The Pattamukkil family used to manage the affairs of the Niranam church in the past. The house was still occupied by members of this ancient family. Another ancient presence was that of a Nasrani sthambam, which was a large open air rock cross, in the compound. The cross was distinctly of Indian design. The edges of the cross was floral and there was a lotus beneath the cross. The church also preserved some body parts of St. Thomas inside it. There was a museum with old artifacts.

Tara returned home convinced that St. Thomas had, indeed, come to Kerala. Her family had told her time and again that they were converted by St. Thomas himself. Tara was cynical. But now there was a story to chase. Tara decided to visit the rest of the eight churches build by St. Thomas. Tara's mother was happy to join her on the trip. Soon, Tara left with her mother to Kerala on her favorite train, the Parashuram express. After snacking on pazham poris and parippu vadas, they arrived at Trissur station.

Everything about Trissur was clean. They traveled from Trissur to Kodungallur by car. They stopped briefly at Guruvayoor temple. Like the sabarimala temple, the Guruvayoor temple was very famous. However, the temple was off limits for non-Hindus. Tara did not want to offend anyone so she decided not to enter the temple. However, Tara was happy to visit both Sabarimala and Guruvayoor. Like the festival of Onam, these places were an integral part of her upbringing. Tara thought that, these brief stops in her journey, were signs of grand things to come.

Following the trail of St. Thomas, Tara made another stop at Palayur. The Palayur church was a modern building. However, some pillars, parts, and foundation stones of the old church were preserved in the church museum. There was a stone cross and some stone lamps in the spot St. Thomas had placed a cross. St. Thomas is said to have converted some Brahmins to Christianity, in Palayur, by performing the water droplets in the air miracle. The Baptismal pond used by St. Thomas was still there. Before leaving, Tara and her mother had lunch at the church canteen.

After Palayur, Tara and her mother finally arrived at Kodungallur. This was where St. Thomas first landed in India. Kodungallur was an important port in ancient times. Part of Kodungallur had gone under the sea resulting in Kodungallur losing prominence to Cochin. Tara and her mother stayed at Hotel Ashwathy which was very close to the Kodungallur Bhagavathy temple. They feasted on fish at every meal. Delicious food was available everywhere in Kerala. They went to the Azhikode beach in the evenings to see the sun set. This is where the river Periyar met the Arabian sea. This confluence of water bodies made trade possible for Kerala with the middle east, enabling St. Thomas to travel to India in merchant boats. The river Periyar was also an important element of St. Thomas's voyage within Kerala.

Tara went to the Bhagavati temple every morning and evening for darshan. The Bhagavati temple was a powerful and famous temple dedicated to Goddess Kali. It was a spacious temple with tiled roofs. Tara also visited the Thiruvanchikulam Mahadeva temple, which is one of the oldest Shiva temples in South India. Shiva is supposed to have resided here with his family. This temple has reference in old Tamil Sangam literature well before the language Malayalam was formed. At these temples, Tara saw people doing the Para vayipadu, which was the practice of weighing people against food and giving it as offerings to God. Tara was seeing a lot of rituals, about which she had heard from her Hindu neighbors, for the first time. The temples like the Kerala palaces were not build to impress but for purpose. The temples were kept thriving, through the ages, by enduring faith.

Tara and her mother, also visited the Cheraman Juma masjid, which is the first mosque in Asia build during Prophet Mohammed's time. Thus, Kodungallur also hosted the first Muslims of the world. Tara followed tradition and offered some silk, incense sticks, and oil as offerings at the mosque. Kodungallur was, indeed, a town of many firsts.

The Kodungallur St. Thomas church was the first church build by St. Thomas in India. It was a beautiful church on the banks of the river Periyar. The bone of the right arm of St. Thomas was kept under lock and key at the altar. This bone was displayed, occasionally, to the public. The lady in charge of the church, for some unknown reason, decided to open the lock and show Tara the bone. It was one of the most amazing moments of Tara's life. A very intense energy hit her. Perhaps it was a blessing or it was love. Something definitely emerged from that bone. Tara thought that if a mere bone had this power, the man St. Thomas might have been so much more charismatic. No wonder wherever he went, he was converting people to Christianity in hordes. This was how a person who attained Nirvana would be. Every cell melts in to compassion. Even after death, compassion emanated from St. Thomas. For the first time in her life,

Tara began to understand and appreciate her Christian faith.

Tara traveled from Kodungallur to North Paravur by car and visited the Kottakkavu Mar Thoma Syro-Malabar Church. The church build by St. Thomas was no longer there. However, within the new church premises, there was a baptismal pond which was used by St. Thomas to baptize Jews and Brahmins. There was also an old church which was build in 1308 AD, which was preserved using air conditioning. This church was a good representation of the ancient presence of Christians in Kerala.

After the church visit, Tara proceeded to Kottayil Kovilikam, which was a small hill on the banks of the confluence of three rivers in North Paravur. On this hill, within a circumference of one km there is a synagogue, a mosque, a church, and a temple, depicting the communal harmony of the region. The Kottayil Kovilikam synagogue was the first synagogue Tara had seen in her life. It looked a lot like the churches she was visiting in Kerala. Almost all Indian Jews had left for Israel in recent times. The only Jewish family who lived nearby, rarely, visited the synagogue. The caretaker of the synagogue was not Jewish. Tara tried to visualize the lifestyle of this hill in ancient times. She was sure it was glorious.

Before leaving Kodungallur, Tara and her mom visited the Kodungallur palace called Chirakkal Kovilakam. The palace had tiled roofing and was simple and comfortable like most Kerala palaces. There was nothing gaudy. It was build for just plain clean living. But like other Kerala palaces, it was also two storied. Such buildings required superior engineering and material which, perhaps, only royalty could afford in the past. People still lived in the palace, though there was a modern house next to it. The future king and a prince took Tara around the palace. They were very friendly. The palace was in bad shape and some rooms were off limits because there was a fear of roof collapse. The royalty of Kodungallur was definitely not rich like the rulers of Travancore. Though, they looked after the affairs of the Kodungallur Bhagavathy temple, they did not claim the temple's wealth. They were modest and honest people. The king explained that the Kodungallur rulers never fought wars. They were mostly interested in promoting culture and education.

The rulers of Kodungallur were also called Varmas like the Travancore rulers. Tara realized that Varma was a royal name in Kerala. Tara had met a boy from Kerala called Varma in Mumbai, a few years ago.

"Varma is a north Indian name. How come your name is Varma?" Tara had asked him.

"There are many Varmas in Kerala" the boy had said. He smiled and said nothing more. Only now she realized he might have been a prince.

Tara did not know much about the royalty of Kerala. India was made of different states. The History syllabus for each state was different. Tara had learned about the Mughals, the British, the Rajputs, and Shivaji in school. She only learned about rulers who fought big wars. But she knew nothing about the Varmas of Kerala. She was glad she was getting to know them now. They were fair and just rulers, whose kingdoms attracted new religions from all over the world. Kerala was a place, not to be missed, in ancient times, if you had a new philosophy.

CHAPTER 10

Malayatoor

Tara and her mother headed to Malayatoor from Kodungallur. They stopped at Kalady, which was the birth place of Adi Shankaracharya, who wrote a bhasya on the Bhagavad Geeta. Tara had watched a film in Sanskrit language by G.V. Iyer, that depicted Shankaracharya's life. It was the first movie in India to be made in Sanskrit. Tara had heard famous bhajans composed by Shankaracharya, which were extremely wise and beautiful. The first stop in Kalady was at a tall Stupa, which was a Buddhist monument to Shankaracharya. Tara was surprised to know that Shankaracharya had followers outside India. The steep climb to the top of the Stupa was made easier by intermingling short paths with stairs. After spending some time at the Stupa, they visited the Adi Shankara Janmabhoomi Kshetram which was Shankaracharya's childhood home on the banks of the Purna river.

The Kshetram was closed when Tara first visited. She proceeded to Kothamangalam and did not find the St. Thomas church she was looking for. Tara was a meticulous planner. She had made an extremely rare mistake in her travel plans. She had confused Kokkamangalam with Kothamangalam. But the mistake brought her back to Kalady. And this time the Kshetram was open. It was destined that she pay proper respects at this place. She would meet Shankaracharya at his birth place in Kalady. She would meet him again at his place of death in the Himalayas. And yet again, she would meet him as a Guru when she read his Geeta bhasya. Tara did not know of all that yet. She was simply happy to behold the house she saw in the Sanskrit movie. Inside the center, Tara saw the spot where Shankaracharya was born and the spot where his mother was cremated. She saw the Ghat in the Purna river where a crocodile bit his legs, convincing his mother to give him permission to become a sanyasi. The Kalady visit made Tara interested in studying the life of Shankaracharya, in depth. So many historical figures became factual and familiar, as Tara traveled.

Tara and her mother reached Malayatoor, late in the evening. They stayed at the Pilgrim center, which was managed by the St. Thomas Syro-Malabar church. The church was situated on the banks of the Periyar river. St. Thomas is said to have held prayers at the site of the church. The rooms at the Pilgrim center could have been better. Good food was difficult to find. Only the location of the Pilgrim center was great. It was right next to the church.

By the time St. Thomas reached Malayatoor, he faced hostile natives. Local religious leaders were angry about the large number of conversions that were happening. Kerala villages were ruled by Brahmin families. When St. Thomas converted one family, the whole village, automatically, converted to Christianity. Faced with threats to his life, St. Thomas fled to a hilltop called Kurishumudi, where he spend many days in prayer. On top of this hill is a church thronged by pilgrims, throughout the year.

Tara and her mother went to the Kurishumudi hill the very evening they reached Malayatoor. They spend some time at a chapel at the bottom of the hill. They lit candles and prayed. Tara's mother was very pious and tears flowed from her eyes. Like Tara, her mother could also feel a strong presence of St. Thomas at Kurishumudi. Miracles were happening and prayers were being granted. Tara had a strong urge to climb the Kurishumudi hill, right away. But her mother would not allow Tara to climb alone at night. So, she had to wait till the next morning. Tara observed, all along this trip, how her mother had aged. Her gait was slow and she would tire easily. Also, her mother could not accompany her up the hill. This hill, she had to climb alone.

Back at the Pilgrim center, Tara made an appointment with a rickshaw driver to take her to Kurishumudi hill at 3.30 in the morning. But Tara had to wait outside the center till four, when the rickshaw finally arrived. In the mean time, she decided to visit the church near the Pilgrim center. She noticed that Malayatoor was like a big house. Pilgrims were sleeping everywhere. They were also sleeping in the courtyard of the church. They came from far, especially Tamilnadu, carrying provisions to cook meals on the road. No one cared about comfort in Malayatoor. It was all about climbing the Kurishumudi hill.

When Tara arrived at Kurishumudi at 4.30 in the morning, there was a small crowd already present. The mountain was alive at all times. All night and day, there were people climbing up or down the hill. Toilets and drinking water were available all along the hill. The hill was well lit at night. The fourteen stations of the cross were placed strategically on the hill, all the way to the top. Tara joined a group of people who were singing and praying while climbing the hill. Tara stopped and prayed with them and lit candles at each station of the cross. The familiar Malayalam songs and prayers enriched her experience. She saw many large wooden crosses placed against trees as she climbed higher. These were crosses pilgrims carried during the Easter festival at the church. There was a station where people offered sesame seeds, rice, black pepper, and salt as offerings. At the Kurishumudi church, there was a huge golden cross, representing the golden cross said to have been found by shepherds, after the saint left the hills. She also saw footprints of St. Thomas encased in glass, on the hill. Tara watched the sunrise from the top of the hills. The scenery was breathtaking. She then attended the Sunday morning mass at 7.30. It was customary to have a lunch of rice kanji at the church. Tara did not wait for lunch as her mother was waiting for her at the Pilgrim center. She bought some Chukku coffee and some tapioca chips, instead. It was delicious and exactly what she needed. As she climbed down the hill, it became more and more crowded. When she reached the bottom of the hill, it was bright day light.

St. Thomas also had climbed down the Kurishumudi hill and proceeded to Mylapore in Tamilnadu. Malayatoor was his last stop at Kerala. He was killed in Tamilnadu.

In the evening, Tara and her mother visited another church founded by St. Thomas, namely, the St. Thomas Syro-Malabar Catholic Church in Kokkamangalam. It was a beautiful church on the banks of the Vembanadu lake. There was a large open air cross erected by St. Thomas in the compound of the church. Seven out of the eight churches build by St. Thomas, are in Kerala. Only Arapally is in Tamilnadu. After the Kokkamangalam church visit, Tara had visited seven churches build by St. Thomas. The only church that Tara had missed from the seven and half churches list was at Kollam. This church had completely gone under the sea. There was another church representing the lost church in the vicinity. But Tara decided to skip the Kollam church, for now. She had seen enough to understand the history of her faith. Tara was happy to be a part of the Syro-Malabar church. It was definitely blessed by St. Thomas.

Tara had decided that when a person attained Nirvana, he would personify compassion. St. Thomas was such an example for her. He was met with angry crowds wherever he went. But he continued spreading his religion. He did not hate the people who threw stones at him and wanted him dead. He wanted to save their souls. People were attracted to him, may be, because he performed miracles. Or perhaps he was very charismatic. Or perhaps, they truly found value in Christianity.

St. Thomas was killed in vain. No religion is really threatened by a new faith. Alternatives are necessary to compare and upgrade one's own beliefs and morals. Tara was content with her Christian upbringing. She believed that her parents gave her God so that he would be there when they were no longer there. Whenever she was far from home, the familiar prayers and songs her parents taught her, would always keep her rooted. It reminded her of where she came from and the standards she needed to uphold. Hinduism was given to her by her birth country. The festivals and traditions of Hinduism were uniquely Indian, and represented the very soil and air of India. She had the best of both worlds. She also found both the religions to be close, as though one was derived from the other. Even on the seven and a half churches trip, she witnessed that Nilackal was close to Sabarimala, Kodungallur was close to Guruvayoor, and Malayatoor was close to Kalady. The next destination for Tara was the Himalayas. But Tara was glad she made these trips to Kerala. Not as famous as the

Himalayas, but Kerala was definitely an important stop for spiritual travelers.

A bunch of Tara's maternal cousins, nieces, and aunts joined her on the way back to Mangalore. They also got to enjoy the parippu vadas and pazham poris on the Parashuram express. Once again, a spiritual trip brought Tara closer to her family, this time, her extended family.

CHAPTER 11

Rishikesh

Tara believed that the Himalayas conferred greatness to visitors. Many successful founders of well known companies, like Steve jobs and Mark Zuckerberg had visited the Himalayas in the initial stages of their careers. Famous music groups like the Beatles had spend time in the Himalayas. For Hindus, Gods lived in the Himalayas. It was Devbhoomi, that is, the land of gods. Tara had prepared for the Himalayan trip for two years now. She had meditated regularly and eaten healthy. She was full of anticipation. Something definitely would happen in this journey. Tara figured that, in the very least, the large volume of earth that made up the Himalayas would change her at a molecular level. It made sense that the Indians worshiped large mountains and rivers. The larger they were, the holier they became. Since we were all made of the five elements, namely, earth, water, fire, air, and space, it was at some level, pure physics and chemistry.

Finally, the day arrived for the Himalayan trip. Tara met Jaya at the Bangalore airport. Tara had invited all her school and college friends to come along. No one could make it. It would be just the two friends. Jaya's mother send some coconut rice for Tara. Tara loved the coconut rice Jaya's mom prepared. Tara used to eat large portions of it from Jaya's lunch box, as a child. It was a nice reminder of bygone school days, as Jaya and Tara ate the home made lunch at the airport.

"It is better to make such trips as soon as we can. Later even if we want to, we may not be able to. We are all gaining in age" said Tara.

"I agree. I am so happy that this trip is really happening" said Jaya.

Tara and Jaya were planning to do the Chardham Yatra, which was a visit to the four most holy places in Hinduism, located in the state of Uttrakhand. This was supposed to be a difficult journey and many people became sick at those high altitudes. To acclimatize themselves to the mountains, before the yatra, they decided to spend some time doing a yoga course in Rishikesh. Rishikesh was, after all, the birthplace of yoga.

It took a long time to get to the Parmarth Niketan Ashram in Rishikesh from the Dehradun airport. The mountain roads were small and precarious, and the traffic was slow. Parmarth Niketan was an ashram on the banks of the Ganges. The best part of the ashram was the easy access to the river. After registering for the yoga course and putting their luggages in the room they shared, Jaya and Tara walked to the ghats. They saw the river Ganges again. Unlike Varanasi, here the river was pristine and pure. The water was ice cold and the flow was rapid. At the same time, they also saw the Himalayas, for the first time. Jaya and Tara were thrilled and really happy. They were grateful and felt blessed.

Soon the evening arti to the Ganges began. Every evening, Swami Chidanand Saraswati held artis at the ghats which was streamed live on YouTube. Tara had watched many of these artis online. Now she saw the singers in person. The ghats were crowded with devotees and the environment was filled with melodious bhajans. The place was lit with oil lamps and there was magic in the air. After the arti, Tara and Jaya, offered lit diyas and flowers to the river.

During the five day course, Jaya and Tara spend a lot of time at the ghats. They woke up early and took dips in the Ganga, every morning, before class. Since the waters were fast, they held chains attached to the river banks, while bathing. The ashram provided delicious, healthy, satvik, vegetarian meals to the yoga students. Since breakfast was served only at eight, Tara and Jaya drank hot ginger tea from the street vendors, to get their day started. Every evening, they attended the arti sessions.

The Yoga course students were required to wear only white clothes. It was a small class. They had all their meals together. They learned many Sanskrit mantras during the course. These mantras were at least five thousand years old. Tara found entire philosophies and ancient wisdom packed in to these mantras.

Tara thought the essence of Christianity was to forgive and ask to be forgiven. Tara found this attitude taken a notch further in the Sayana mantra. This mantra asked for forgiveness from the Lord Shiva, who is the ocean of kindness, for any wrong action done, knowingly or unknowingly, through any organs of action (hands, feet, speech) or organs of perception (eyes, ears), or the mind. This mantra was to be recited before going to sleep, every night. Ancient India was not about an eye for an eye, and a tooth for a tooth kind of culture. It was founded on kindness and forgiveness.

Another mantra Tara loved was the Vishnu mantra which said that whatever I do, with my body, speech, mind, sense organs, using my intellect or my intrinsic nature, I offer to the Lord Narayana. Their teacher emphasized how this mantra meant that your life, itself, must be a prayer. Prayers are not limited only to religious rituals. Even sweeping the room should be done with an attitude of prayer.

The Purnam mantra talked about the completeness of God. The Surya Namaskaram mantra and the Om Asatoma mantra asked for the revelation of the truth. The Nirvana Shatakam talked about how we were not the body, the mind, our sins, our good deeds, or our ego. We were Shiva himself. Tara did not understand what many of the mantras were saying. But they sounded beautiful. Tara had an appreciation for the language Sanskrit in her genetics. All Indian languages were derived from Sanskrit. The mantras sounded very familiar, as though she had heard them before. Moreover, during evening artis at the ghats, Tara was happy to recite these newly learned mantras, along with the crowd.

They also learned many asanas in the Yoga course. Tara had a difficult time sitting on the floor with crossed legs. This was the easiest asana called the Sukhasana. Tara was used to sitting on chairs all the time. Simple tasks like sitting on the floor had become difficult for her. Tara had decided after every meditation course, to practice sitting on the floor. But she never got to it. Tara struggled with many asanas but most students were in a worse situation than her. This was an introduction course. Tara and Jaya were among the best students in the class. The reason being that the two friends really put in an effort to learn. Their yoga teacher, however, could perform all kinds of seemingly impossible asanas. But the teacher came to yoga from a history of serious health problems. Yoga had saved her life. Yoga had done, for her, what modern medicine had failed to do. Tara was witnessing a miracle in the form of the yoga teacher.

Every evening, after the arti, Tara attended the satsangs conducted by Sadhvi Bhagawati Saraswati. Tara had watched the story of Sadhvi Saraswati online. The Sadhvi, who was originally from California, was visiting Parmarth Niketan, casually. In that first visit, the Ganges became her God, Swami Chidanand Saraswati became her Guru, and she never left the Ashram. During the satsangs, everyone sang bhajans. Afterwards, the Sadhvi answered questions that were asked by the audience in front of her or the ones that were asked online.

"I know someone who is full of hate and anger towards me. What should I do when he keeps hurting me?" the Sadhvi read out loud, a question someone had asked online. "You should show that person some love. He can only give what he has. This person has only known hurt. He can only give out hurt. Only love can destroy hate. If you show hate to this person, you are only adding to what that person already knows. If you show him some love, there is some hope for change" replied the Sadhvi.

Tara was thinking of how Christ had asked people to love their enemies. The Sadhvi was saying the same thing. This was ancient wisdom. The yoga course was shedding light on principles Tara already followed, and also cultivating some new ones in her.

Tara and Jaya met their classmate, Jai, in Rishikesh. Jai was in Rishikesh on business and he made a brief stop at Parmarth Niketan to see them. He gave them both a copy of the book "The teaching of the Bhagavad Gita" by Swami Dayananda Saraswati. Swami Dayananda Saraswati also had an ashram in Rishikesh. He was Jai's Guru. Jai was in a hurry to visit his Guru's ashram and left soon. Tara felt good to receive that book from Jai, on the banks of the river Ganga. Tara was not planning to read any books for a long time. She was experiencing spirituality, in action, right now. However, she thought it was an appropriate gift.

The yoga class kept Tara and Jaya very busy. They missed one evening arti and visited the Kunjapuri temple which was on top of a hill. It was a long car trip and Jaya chanted the Lalita Sahasranama, which was the thousand different names of Goddess Durga, on the way. They climbed many stairs to reach the temple. Apart from this temple, they did not leave the ashram, throughout the course. They got late when they got back to the Ashram. Their friends had saved dinner for them. The class had become a family. They were sad to part when the course was over.

On the last day of the course, after the morning yoga session, the students were allowed to do whatever they pleased. But the very same day, there was a taxi strike in the city. Tara and Jaya had to take a rickshaw to go to the GMVN office to register for the Chardham yatra which would begin the next day. GMVN was a government organization in charge of travel within Uttrakhand. The rickshaw ride was not comfortable because the mountain roads were rough. Tara decided to proceed to Haridwar by rickshaw. Jaya went back to the Ashram. Haridwar was a big city and the Ganges at Haridwar was wide and impressive. Tara decided to visit the Mansa Devi and Chandi Devi temples. The rickshaw driver came along with Tara as guide. It would have been impossible for Tara to find her way, otherwise. There was a long walk to the Mansa Devi temple ticket counter. She even had to take a cycle rickshaw part of the way. The ticket counter was crowded and her guide arranged for tickets for the two temples. Tara had to take a sky lift to reach the temples. There were huge lines for darshan and the security was tight. All wishes were supposedly granted at these temples. But Tara felt silly wishing for anything. In the grand scheme of things, begging for personal wishes to be granted seemed so wrong. She prayed for the world in general.

After the temple visits, Tara headed for Har ki Pauri. This was believed to be the precise place where the Ganges enters the plains. Taking a dip at Har ki Pauri was a ritual to follow for a successful Chardham trip. At around eight in the night, Tara took a dip at Har ki Pauri before going back to Rishikesh. It was late when Tara reached the ashram. Jaya had saved dinner for Tara.

Jaya had spend the day doing laundry and was bored. Almost all the students had left and Jaya was alone. She wished she had joined Tara on the Haridwar trip. When the laundry was dry, Jaya decided to fold and pack them. She saw some extra clothes that were not hers, drying in the clotheslines. Jaya decided to fold them too, thinking that they were Tara's clothes. Suddenly, the only other student left in the ashram, a German gentleman appeared before Jaya. He scooped up his clothes, gave Jaya some dirty looks, and left without a word. All the clothes students wore were white. It was a valid mistake on Jaya's part.

"He thought I was stealing his clothes" Jaya said sheepishly, when she met Tara.

"Yes. Waiting till the last day for opportunity, when everyone was gone" said Tara laughing.

The two friends talked of what might have gone on in the German gentleman's mind, and laughed for a long time. They had to wake up early the next morning. It was time for the Chardham trip.

CHAPTER 12

The Chardham Yatra

The taxi strike continued on the day the Chardham trip began. GMVN employees came to see Jaya and Tara off. It was rare that two women would embark on such a monumental journey, on their own. The GMVN employees wanted to make them feel secure and confident. Tara and Jaya had to cross the Ramjhoola bridge across the river to reach a car parked discretely at a place away from the Ashram to avoid any trouble. The GMVN employees introduced them to their driver Keerti Singh and wished them luck. The two friends were happy to be on the road, far away from taxi strikes.

"At GMVN we know how to get you there. Relax" said Keerti Singh.

Tara and Jaya were really in good hands. Keerti Singh had saved pilgrims assigned to him during the Kedarnath floods. He regularly took pilgrims on the Chardham yatra. The Chardham yatra was really about the origins of the rivers Ganga and Yamuna. The four dhams (holy places) were Yamunotri, Gangotri, Kedarnath, and Badrinath. The first dham was Yamunotri which was the origin of the river Yamuna. Yamuna was considered the second most holy river in India, next only to Ganga. Yamuna would, eventually, join Ganga in Triveni Sangam at Allahabad. The rivers that originated from the other three dhams, Bhagirathi from

Gangotri, Mandakini from Kedarnath, and Alaknanda from Badrinath, merged to form the river Ganga, at Devaprayag.

Keerti Singh took a slightly longer route to get to Yamunotri to avoid traffic. He stopped at Hilton, a Five star hotel, for a toilet break. Jaya decided to get breakfast, too. It was a buffet and no one was particularly hungry. They were served a whopping bill as they were leaving. Jaya and Tara decided that Five star hotels were not a great idea on this trip. That kind of lavish spending did not align with the spirit of this yatra. Moreover, nothing about the meal stood out, apart from the price.

The route to Yamunotri was scenic. It was a beautiful sunny day. They made a brief stop at Mussorie which was very touristy. Tara rented some colorful local costumes and took pictures. It felt like she was on a holiday and not a pilgrimage. But soon, Tara and Jaya were thrilled to see the river Yamuna for the first time. They stopped and paid homage to the river. Keerti singh hurried them, warning them of the dangers of the mountain roads. Landslides and flash floods were frequent.

They Reached Janaki Chatti late in the evening. Keerti Singh would stay back in the car in a parking area and socialize with other car drivers. Tara and Jaya had to walk a long way, uphill, to reach the GMVN guest house at Janaki Chatti. A porter carried their luggage to their room. They were tired and it was a cold night. They were served a warm dinner of rotis, rice, dal, paneer, and sabji. Food at GMVN guest houses was vegetarian, healthy, and delicious. Tara and Jaya made arrangements for pony rides in the morning to the Yamunotri temple, before they slept.

The geysers were not working. The hotel management provided buckets of hot water to people who asked for it.

However, Tara took a cold water shower in the morning. She had no fear of cold water after her Ganga dips at Rishikesh. Tara and Jaya rode ponies to the Yamunotri temple early morning. The owners of the ponies walked along, controlling the animals and acting as tour guides. On the way, they stopped at the Bhairava temple and Jaya offered prayers. Bhairava was believed to protect the dangerous road to the Yamunotri temple, the pilgrims, and even the temple.

The Yamunotri temple was a beautiful temple situated on the banks of river Yamuna surrounded by hills. At the temple, a friendly young priest did Puja for a fee. He cooked some rice in Suryakund, which was a hot water spring in the temple premises. He gave the rice to Tara and Jaya and asked them to feed it to birds. He also collected cans of fresh Yamuna water and gave it to the two friends. Tara had plenty of things to carry back.

There were many food stalls outside the Yamunotri temple. To Tara's utter disappointment, Maggi noodles was the most common dish served at every stall. Jaya opted for a bowl of warm Maggi noodles. Tara wanted to eat authentic local food. She tried some aloo parathas and jilebis made on firewood which was not so great. Good local food was difficult to find. Even at GMVN guest houses, there were no local dishes served. Tara needed to find some way to eat local food. Visiting a place would be incomplete if she did not eat the produce of the place.

Tara wanted to walk part of the way to the temple. She wanted to use the pony only as a backup. Her guides discouraged her from walking citing time constraints. On the way back from the temple, Tara insisted on walking. After a few steps she fell flat on the ground. She slipped on some pony dung. Also, it was not fun to walk with heavy pony traffic, going both ways, on the narrow road. Tara gave up walking and got back on the pony quickly. The pony ride from Janaki Chatti to Yamunotri was a total of Twelve Kilometers to and fro. It was a difficult ride. Her backsides hurt. But the ride was a good sampler to what the pony ride to Kedarnath would be which was Sixteen Kilometers from Gaurikund. Tara was convinced that the Kedarnath journey would hurt a little, but was surely doable, after the Yamunotri experience.

Gangotri was the next dham on the Chardham list. It was a two day journey with a stop in Barkot. Barkot was a small, beautiful, warm town. Janaki Chatti was cold but Barkot was warm and comfortable. Tara tried some local sweets at Barkot which were really good. The Himalayan cattle milk was definitely special, if not holy. Apart from tea, sweets were another way of tasting some Himalayan milk. Tara saw trees from which tar was extracted from for the first time at Barkot. On the way to Gangotri, Tara mentioned that they had not seen any real local food to Keerti Singh. From then on, Keerti Singh made it a point to stop at small dhabas that served authentic and fresh local food. Thus, they got to eat Fiddlehead Fern called lengda, for the first time. Lengda grew in the wild and tasted a lot like asparagus. They ate mooli parathas and sabji made from freshly plucked, locally grown radishes. They ate dal chawal with slices of onion like the locals. Thus, Keerti Singh introduced them to simple, non touristy delicious food.

A hot spring source was associated with every dham. Rishikund was a hot spring located in the middle of the city of Gangnani. Tara and Jaya stopped to take a bath at Gangnani before proceeding to the Gangotri. There were separate areas for bathing for men and women. The hot spring water pools were located inside a building and was not particularly interesting. But Tara and Jaya decided to follow the ritual of bathing at the Rishikund before proceeding to the Gangotri dham.

It is believed that King Bhagiratha prayed for Ganga to come down to earth from heaven. Hence the river at the Gangotri dham is called Bhagirathi and according to mythology, considered the source stream of the river Ganges. All the dhams were cold and Gangotri was no exception. But Jaya wanted to take a dip at Bhagirathi since it was so religiously significant. Tara and Jaya watched how other people poured mugs of water over themselves instead of immersing themselves in the river. They decided to do the same in the morning. They attended evening arti at the Gangotri temple. There was a small group of people present at the temple at that hour. Way up in the mountains, these people had come from far to worship the divine. There was an unspoken camaraderie as they waited for the arti to begin. After the temple arti, Tara and Jaya joined the evening arti to the Bhagirathi river at the Ghats. They walked back to the guest house to eat a warm vegetarian dinner of rotis, dal, and sabji.

Next morning, a shopkeeper on the banks of the river gave plastic mugs to Tara and Jaya for the Bhagirathi bath ritual.

"The river currents are fast. Hold on to your mugs tightly" the shopkeeper warned.

But the minute Tara placed the mug in the river, it was gone. "I told you to watch out" said the shopkeeper and gave Tara another mug.

This time Tara was better. Tara realized that it was a lot easier to pour mugs of ice cold water over the head when compared to taking dips. Jaya was really happy and was chanting all kinds of prayers. When Tara offered money to the shopkeeper for the lost mug, he would not take any. Tara bought a small copper pot from the shopkeeper as a memento.

After the temple visit, Tara and Jaya walked to the Pandava Gufa, which was a cave in which Pandavas stayed for some time. A Sadhu had been living in that cave for twelve years. He offered to make tea which Jaya accepted. Jaya asked him to share wisdom while he was making tea. The Sadhu said reciting the Hanuman Chalisa would give solution to all worldly problems. Jaya wanted the Sadhu to recite the Hanuman Chalisa. The Sadhu refused a few times but Jaya persevered. Tara was surprised when the Sadhu finally recited the prayers. She was sure he would not oblige but Jaya had managed to convince him.

Tara and Jaya, slowly, walked a long way back to the GMVN guest house. From Varanasi days, it was clear that the two ladies felt at home everywhere they went. They were definitely at home in the beautiful Himalayas. As soon as they got back to their room, it was time to pack and leave Gangotri. They were headed for the Kedarnath dham. However, there would be two more night stops, namely, Uttarkashi and Guptkashi, before Kedarnath. The sun shone bright as Keerti Singh drove across the mountains filled with rice terraces and farm houses. The Uttarakhand women were strikingly beautiful, strong, and hard working. Tara and Jaya stopped and talked to local women they met on the road carrying firewood or grass for cattle, in baskets on their backs. They ate at roadside dhabas and stopped at waterfalls. Every evening they arrived early at a GMVN guesthouse and got plenty of rest. There was nothing to complain about. Tara and Jaya were in a constant state of bliss.

They visited the Kashivishwanath temples at Uttarkashi and Guptkashi. Shiva is believed to have gone in to hiding as a bull, to avoid the Pandavas, at Guptkashi. Pandavas wanted forgiveness from Shiva for the Mahabarath battle which Shiva was reluctant to give. Also, Shiva is believed to have proposed to Parvati at Guptkashi. Hence, Guptkashi temple definitely was an important one. They also visited the Agastya Muni ashram on the way to Guptkashi. Agastya Muni, who was the author of many hymns in the Rigveda, is believed to have meditated at this ashram.

Keerti Singh made sure that all the important places that came in a typical Chardham yatra were covered. Tara was experiencing significant religious history without much time for processing. All she could clearly remember was how the weather was exceptionally good and how everything was extremely pleasant. The Himalayan roads surrounded by imposing rocks, with very little traffic, felt like a pathway to heaven. Finally, the day of the trip to Kedarnath arrived.

CHAPTER 13

Kedarnath

The destruction brought on by the 2013 Kedarnath floods was raw in everyone's memory in Uttarakhand. Tara had seen the news of the flood on the internet. It was the first time she had heard about the Kedarnath temple. She had wanted to visit Kedarnath from that time onwards. It was a compelling pull she had felt. It was five years since the floods. The morning was bright and sunny as they headed towards Kedarnath.

Jaya decided to take the helicopter to Kedarnath temple and Tara decided to ride the pony. Their decision was based on the Yamunotri pony ride experience. Both, Tara and Jaya knew it was not an easy ride. After seeing Jaya off at the Sersi Helipad, Keerti Singh found a horseman to take Tara to Kedarnath. Keerti Singh would wait for them at Sersi. Kedarnath was generally considered to be the toughest journey of the Chardham yatra. Tara was on her own now. She took a ride to Gaurikund in a jeep full of strangers. Before the Kedarnath dham yatra, it was tradition to take a dip at the hot water spring at Gaurikund. However, the Kedarnath flood had destroyed all man made facilities. Tara decided to just sprinkle some water over her head before heading towards the pony that was waiting for her. It would have been great if she had more time to explore Gaurikund. She saw bitter gourd served in restaurants. Any place that could sell bitter gourd in street shops was definitely worth exploring. But there was no time to waste. Sixteen kilometers were to be covered and the weather was unpredictable.

The horseman walked along, acting as a guide, as Tara rode the pony. Some paths were steep and if the pony decided to buckle, Tara would fall down to a certain death. At Rishikesh, a fellow student from the Yoga course had narrated how he had injured himself, after falling from a pony enroute to Kedarnath. But Tara was not thinking about the dangerous road. She was expecting God to manifest on that road. Besides, her mind was occupied with the pain she was feeling on her behind. She asked her guide to take a break, several times, but he continued on. Each time, he promised to take a break soon which seldom happened. He did take two short breaks for tea and lunch, when he also attended to the needs of his pony. Tara really appreciated those breaks. During the breaks, Tara took deep breaths of the mountain air and watched pilgrims make their journey. It was a busy road. There were pilgrims walking to Kedarnath. Others were riding ponies. And yet, others were being carried in baskets on people's backs. No matter what your age or health status was, there were means to get to Kedarnath.

Tara saw divine kindness on those hills. Kind humans who helped pilgrims to get to Kedarnath. Interestingly, most of the guides were Muslims. Tara was surprised to find that Muslims were such an important component of one of the holiest Hindu pilgrimages. Tara's guide's name did not register in Tara's memory, but it was definitely a Muslim name. The pony ride was difficult for her while her guide was walking all the way. He definitely was strong and showed no sign of tiredness. After a while, Tara stopped asking for breaks and listened to the silence of the mountains. The pilgrims in Kedarnath were not a noisy bunch. The weather was excellent and in no time the five hour ride came to an end.

"Here is your stop" said the guide.

"Thank you" said Tara as she climbed down. She was very tired.

"I will carry your bag but I will walk ahead. I need to see if I can find any tourists who want a ride back to Gaurikund" said the guide.

"Okay. Thank you" said Tara. She started walking towards the GMVN camp at Kedarnath. She tired easily and sat down a few times. It was only a couple of kilometers to her residence but Tara found it difficult to walk. Perhaps, it was due to the low oxygen levels at that height. But slowly and surely, Tara made it to her destination. Her guide handed her, her bag and bid her goodbye. He understood she was tired. He was not judging but was, instead, helping her. He was happy that they made it to Kedarnath, without any problems. Anything could have gone wrong. It was no mean task.

"Did you find a tourist to take back to Gaurikund?" asked Tara.

"Yes" said the guide as he hurried back to his pony. He had tied his pony and given it grass and water as soon as they arrived. Tara was really grateful to the kind stranger who made this momentous journey possible for her.

The day Tara and Jaya arrived at Kedarnath was also the International Yoga day. The guards stationed at Kedarnath learned that Jaya had come from Rishikesh after attending a yoga course. They asked Jaya to conduct a yoga session for them. Thus, Jaya had spend the morning teaching yoga to some army men. Jaya was thrilled and was eager to narrate her experience to Tara as soon as she saw her. They had an excellent lunch of rotis, dal, rice, and sabji prepared by volunteers. And then Tara slept for a few hours.

When Tara, finally, woke up, she was ready to explore Kedarnath. She was fully energized as she walked towards the Kedarnath temple. She stopped at the Mandakini river that flowed near the temple. It looked gentle and small, almost like a stream. But, this river had flooded and destroyed lives and property all along Uttarakhand. It was too cold to take a dip. So Tara sprinkled some water on her head and wet her face. Then, she saw the Jyothirlingam at the temple for the first time. The floods, that created so much havoc, did not destroy the temple. In fact, the flood waters brought a huge rock, which was later named Bheem shila, and placed it in front of the temple in such a way, that the waters flowed from the sides of the rock, protecting the temple. Nature protected the temple, that fateful day, but destroyed everything else in the vicinity. Tara also saw Shankaracharya's Samadhi near the Bheem Shila. She was reminded of his birthplace in Kerala. The floods had destroyed his Samadhi and his final resting place was marked only by a picture. But it definitely was a holy spot and Tara paid her respects to the great man.

Late in the evening, Tara and Jaya went back to the temple for arti. As they waited for the arti to begin, someone started chanting Om. Everyone chanted along. When the chanting stopped Jaya started leading the Om chants. The entire temple reverberated with Om chants. Kedarnath was prompting Jaya to lead, a second time that very same day. After the arti, Jaya and Tara walked back to the GMVN guest house, and had a warm dinner. In the night, it got very cold and Tara could not sleep. The thick blanket the guesthouse provided was of no help. Tara wished she had spend the night at the temple instead of trying to sleep in vain. There were programs, all night, at the temple. Tara decided if she ever visited Kedarnath again, she would not waste time trying to sleep.

In the morning, when Tara went for darshan, a priest offered to do puja for a fee. He applied a lot of fragrant pastes and ash on Tara's forehead. Then he asked Tara to apply ghee to the lingam. This was the first time Tara had touched a shiva lingam at a temple. The holiest lingam in India was accessible to the common person. You could touch it. It was personal. You could also sit in the sanctum sanctorum as long as you wanted. This was different from any temple Tara had visited so far. It was free and liberating.

It was soon time to leave Kedarnath. Both, Jaya and Tara took the helicopter back to Sersi. There was no more time for pony rides. They reached Sersi in a matter of minutes. Nothing was guaranteed in Kedarnath. If the weather was cloudy, helicopters would not fly for days. But Jaya and Tara had met there schedule without any problems. Tara contemplated on what the Kedarnath trip did for her. Though she could not say that God manifested himself, she did witness the divine in the kindness of people and nature. The sunny days on the Chardham trip like the Bheem Shila were all blessings of nature.

CHAPTER 14

Badrinath

Keerti Singh met Jaya and Tara at Sersi helipad and drove them to the Triyuginarayan temple where it is believed that Shiva and Parvati got married. Jaya's Guru had asked her to visit this temple and chant a list of mantras. Jaya sat, with her eyes closed, for more than an hour, and chanted away the mantras. She kept swatting flies away from her face as she prayed. Jaya was always generous with her prayers. She prayed for her friends, family, and the world in general. The food offerings attracted flies at the temple but no one was bothered by it. Flies were also god's creation and were accepted at that place. Tara walked around the temple a bit and then sat next to Jaya and waited for her to finish her prayers. She could not yet come to terms with the fact that the Kedarnath dham was done. Now only, the Badrinath dham was left.

As Tara left the Triyuginarayan temple, she could sense an intense joy engulfing her entire being.

"The austere and difficult part of the Chardham is over. Now, we are heading towards abundance" explained Jaya.

The three main deities of Hinduism were Brahma, the creator, Vishnu, the sustainer, and Shiva, the destroyer. Brahma's wife was Saraswati, who was the goddess of knowledge, Vishnu's wife was Laxmi, who was the goddess of wealth, and Shiva's wife was Parvati, who was the goddess of power. To create, you need knowledge, to sustain, you need resources, and to destroy you need power. Thus, wives held powerful portfolios in Hinduism providing their husbands, the necessary tools to perform their duties. The idea that behind every successful man was a woman was the very essence of Hindu philosophy.

It was believed that, Kedarnath represented Shiva, thereby, austerity, and Badrinath represented Vishnu, and hence abundance. Whatever the reasons, Tara felt an abundance of joy. It was not clear that it was because she came from Kedarnath or whether it was because she was heading for Badrinath. To match Tara's mood, the weather was sunny and cheerful as well.

Tara and Jaya had to stop for the night at Tilwara before the Badrinath dham. They reached Tilwara GMVN late in the evening. The only guests, that night, were Jaya and Tara. The bus load of guests who were to arrive that day were delayed because of a landslide. Tara and Jaya did their laundry there. This was the only time in the whole Chardham yatra, they found time to do laundry. There were no clotheslines to dry their clothes. The hotel staff asked them to hang it on railings, since there were no other guests. Thus, washed clothes were hung all over the building.

Tilwara GMVN was situated on the banks of the Mandakini river that originated at Kedarnath. Tara spend a lot of time besides the river. It was as though her time with Kedarnath was extended. Tilwara GMVN was her favorite guesthouse in the entire trip. Tara kept mentioning about the good energy she felt there. In the morning, the hotel staff took her to the Lat baba samadhi situated within the premises of the guesthouse. Lat baba was a holy man and

Tara realized his grave was generating the good energy she was experiencing, all along.

The sun shone bright in the sky as Tara and Jaya left Tilwara for Badrinath. Their first stop was at Karnaprayag, which was the confluence of the rivers Pindar and Alaknanda. Prayag meant a confluence of rivers. Karnaprayag was one of the five main prayags in the Chardham yatra. It is believed that Karna of Mahabharata meditated at this confluence and acquired the protective gears of Kavacha (armour) and Kundala (earrings), from his father, the Sun God. They had seen Sonprayag, only from far, on the way to Kedarnath. After visiting Karnaprayag, Tara asked Keerti Singh to make sure they did not miss any more prayags. The confluences of rivers were chosen places by sages and Gods for meditation. Tara also wanted to meditate here and figure if the place made any difference. She wanted to spend quality time at the prayags.

The next stop was at the river Garud Ganga, which was said to be the only river that flowed in the northward direction to merge with Alaknanda. It was tradition to worship Garuda at the temple near the banks of Garud Ganga, before the Badrinath dham. This temple was considered the gateway to Badrinath. At this place, Garuda had meditated to eradicate his ego. After he completed his meditation, Vishnu is believed to have blessed every stone at the bank of the river. Tara and Jaya had not heard of Garud Ganga. They were there because Keerti Singh brought them there. But Jaya was fascinated by the idol of Garuda at the temple and she asked plenty of questions to the priest at the temple. As a result, the priest did many rites and gave Tara and Jaya some stones to take back home. It was tradition to take back stones from the river. Tara and Jaya, thus, fulfilled tradition, without realizing it, because of Jaya's fascination of Garuda. On the other hand, Tara was fascinated by the Common Peacock butterfly she saw at Garud Ganga. She stood there, by the river, watching this lone butterfly for a long time. Common Peacock was the state butterfly of Uttarakhand. This butterfly with the colors of Krishna felt like a message from the universe that God was with them on the journey to Badrinath.

The next stop that day was at Joshimatt where Shankaracharya lived for several years. By this time, Tara's appreciation of Shankaracharya had grown manifold. Shankaracharya had installed the Vishnu statue at Badrinath, where they were headed.

After Joshimatt, they stopped at Vishnuprayag, where the rivers Dhouli Ganga from Tibet and Alaknanda merged. Here, it was believed that Narad Muni meditated and Vishnu appeared before him. There were buckets attached to chains for people who wanted to do the bath rituals. The water was very fast flowing and a little scary. A priest poured buckets of water over Tara. There was no place nor time to change. It was evening and Tara was shivering a little. She did not linger long at the Hanuman temple which was the last stop before the Badrinath GMVN.

Tara and Jaya quickly got ready to explore the Badrinath temple. Vapors from the Tapt Kund, which is a hot water sulfur spring, could be seen as they entered the temple. Tara and Jaya followed tradition and took a bath at the Tapt kund before entering the temple. They waited to attend the Sayana arti which was the ritual of putting the gods to sleep. Jaya shed tears of joy. Jaya belonged to the community that worshiped Vishnu. Hence, Badrinath was the highest dham for her. The only person in her immediate family to have visited Badrinath was her grandfather. Jaya's father called to congratulate her. The next morning, Tara and Jaya went back to the temple and offered flowers and prayers. They spend some time by the river Alaknanda. Then, they started to head back to Rishikesh. Chardham was over. Everything had gone far better than planned. Tara and Jaya felt blessed.

CHAPTER 15

The River Sarasvati

The first stop after leaving Badrinath was at the Mana village, which was located at the border of India and China, and hence was known as the last village of India. Keerti Singh stayed back at the parking lot as Tara and Jaya walked towards the village. Tara saw domestic yaks for the first time in her life. The people of Mana village herded yaks. They also sold hand knitted items to visitors. Tara bought woolen socks as gifts for her parents. She also bought some holy sticks that was supposed to have the power to ward off evil. The lady who sold these items invited Tara and Jaya to her home and showed them how they lived. She gave them incense cones she made herself from herbs and dung. She refused to take any money for it. The people who lived here were simple and wanted little.

Tara did not know then, but Mana village would turn out to be one of the most important stops in the Chardham yatra. The epic Mahabarata was composed here in a cave called the Ganesh Gufa by Lord Ganesh under the instructions of Sage Vyasa. The great Sage Vyasa who composed the Vedas, Puranas, and the Mahabarata, lived here in a cave called Vyasa Gufa. Tara and Jaya visited the Ganesh Gufa and the Vyasa Gufa. Tara tried to picture Sage Vyasa writing away on palm leaves, five thousand years ago. It was difficult to

process that era of greatness but Tara was glad she got to see the caves.

A holy man who was giving sermons at the Vyasa Gufa told them about Vasundara falls. The water of Vasundara falls refuses to fall on people who are not pure of heart. But it was a steep climb to Vasundara falls. The Pandavas had gone that way to Swargarohini glacier, which was believed to be the stairway to heaven. Tara and Jaya did not have time for that hike in this trip. They decided to finish the tour of Mana village quickly.

Soon they spotted the Sarasvati river which was considered the fourth holiest river in India. The source of the Sarasvati river was at the Mana village. The mantra, Hindus recite, while bathing, mentions seven holy rivers, in their order of importance, and goes thus,

"Gange ca Yamune caiva Godavari Sarasvati Narmade Sindhu Kaveri jalesmin sannidhim kuru."

The mantra asks the seven holy rivers, Ganga, Yamuna, Godavari, Sarasvati, Narmada, Sindhu, and Kaveri to be present in the water used in bathing. Tara and Jaya had seen the source of Godavari at Nashik. In the Chardham yatra they visited the source of Yamuna and Ganga. Here they met the source of the river Sarasvati without having planned it. Tara was thrilled. Jaya and Tara had covered the sources of the four most holy rivers of India. Moreover, Sarasvati river could only be seen at the Mana village. Sarasvati river vanishes underground and resurfaces only at Allahabad to join Ganga and Yamuna. Even at Allahabad, Sarasvati river is not visible.

But here, in Mana village, the Sarasvati river was roaring. A huge single rock bridge that went across the Sarasvati river

was called the Bheem bridge. It was believed to be placed there by the Pandavas on their way to Swargarohini. Tara and Jaya paid their respects at the Sarasvati temple and checked out the many tea shops, all of which claimed to be the last tea shop of India. Tara wanted to sprinkle water from the Sarasvati river on her head. Sarasvati is the Hindu goddess of knowledge and the river was named after her. Tara decided that the river definitely had something to do with knowledge because in her vicinity, the Mahabarata was composed.

The path to the river was steep and not easily accessible. Jaya, who had walked ahead of Tara, had already sprinkled some water, fetched by local boys, on herself. Local boys were running up and down the steep path and providing Sarasvati water for visitors. But Tara wanted to touch the river. One local boy told her if she kept walking, there would be a place where she could touch the river. Tara told Jaya about it and asked her to join her. But Jaya was already done with her sprinkling ritual and she decided to walk back. So Tara walked alone for a long time. From the other side of the river people watched as Tara walked alone on the path. Tara was the only visitor walking on that path, that day. After a couple of kilometers the path reached the waters.

Tara was very happy. She sat down and ran her fingers through the Sarasvati river for a long time. This represented the river of knowledge for Tara. Tara noticed another stream of water joining the river. Suddenly, out of nowhere, two local boys appeared where Tara was sitting. She asked them about the stream and they told her it was the waters that came from the Vasundara falls. Tara was thrilled and quickly sprinkled water from Vasundara falls on herself. The waters of the Vasundara falls was believed to grant moksha, liberation. It was believed that only good people got to touch this water. Tara was at the spot where the Vasundara falls and Sarasvati river merged. Later, Tara would learn from the Bhagvad Gita, that the definition of attaining moksha was gaining knowledge about Brahman. Thus, chasing knowledge would lead to moksha. Tara had chased the river Sarasvati and reached the waters of the Vasundara falls. It was somehow symbolic.

Tara loved that spot and wished Jaya could have experienced it too. But the mobile phone was out of range and time was flying. Tara started walking back. Tara stopped at a fountain in the rock, where the water was believed to come from Kailash Mansarovar in Tibet. Tara quickly sprinkled some water from the fountain on herself and walked along. Tara was eager to tell Jaya about her experience. She was surprised that Jaya had witnessed Tara reaching the river Sarasvati and the Vasundara stream from the opposite side of the river. Jaya had even taken a picture of her. Jaya knew everything already and there was nothing to add.

"You should have come if you knew that the Vasundara falls water was accessible there. In fact, you go and come. I will wait" said Tara.

"Another time" said Jaya.

Jaya always thought there was another time. Tara always thought this was it. Life flows fast and Tara rarely had the opportunity nor the will to go back to a place again.

Jaya had arranged for mooli parathas to be made at a restaurant. The two friends had a delicious lunch, together, at Mana village. Soon they bid farewell to the Mana village which could easily be considered as the fifth dham, because it was the origin of the Sarasvati river.

CHAPTER 16

Devaprayag

It was late evening when they reached the Rudraprayag GMVN guest house. At Rudraprayag, the rivers Mandakini from Kedarnath and Alaknanda from Badrinath met. Tara and Jaya could see this confluence from their room's balcony. It was a blessed evening and it felt like everything was right with the universe. In the morning, Jaya and Tara walked down a rough path, to take a dip at a point where the waters of the two rivers mixed. Soon after breakfast they were on the road again. This was the last day of the Chardham yatra.

Their first stop was at the Rudraprayag temple where Narad Muni is believed to have meditated. The temple was located at the confluence of the rivers Alaknanda and Mandakini. The waters of Mandakini was greenish and that of Alaknanda was white. The rivers met gently and the waves seemed to caress each other. At this place, the two rivers met, at every instant of time, for thousands of years, in this same gentle manner. It was definitely a place of joy for Tara. It was definitely worth exploring why such confluences were chosen places for meditation by Gods, Kings, and Sages.

After the Rudraprayag temple, Keerti Singh took them to Dhari devi temple, which was located on the banks of the Alaknanda river, in Srinagar. Disturbing Dhari devi idol from it's original location for the construction of a dam is believed to have caused Kedarnath floods. Hours after the idol was moved, floods and landslides devastated Kedarnath killing hundreds of people. A similar attempt in the past by a local king is believed to have resulted in major landslides at Kedarnath.

Could nature get angry? The Kedarnath temple suffered only minor damages during the floods. Nature had placed the rock, Bhim shila, strategically, to protect the temple. The way the rivers met at the confluences, like long lost friends, made Tara think they were conscious. In this trip, nature appeared more and more conscious and responsive to Tara.

They stopped for lunch in Srinagar at Chauhan Bengali sweets. They feasted on momos, sweets, and lassi. Everyone was in a great mood when they reached Devaprayag. At Devaprayag, Bageerati from Gangotri merges with Alaknanda from Badrinath and the resulting river is known as Ganga. The waters of Bhageerati was brown and the waters of Alaknanda was white. At all the confluences of Alaknanda before, even at Rudraprayag, the river continued on as Alaknanda. But at Devaprayag, Alaknanda loses identity to become Ganga. By now, the three main source rivers Bageerati, Mandakini, and Alaknanda have merged to form Ganga.

At Devaprayag, Tara and Jaya first paid respects to a temple dedicated to Lord Ram. Lord Ram is said to have meditated here. Then they proceeded to take their holy dips at Devaprayag. A priest performed traditional rituals before they took their dips. The water was fast flowing. They had to hold on to chains for safety. After the ice cold water dips, Tara and Jaya sat in the warm sun to dry. The Chardham yatra had taken them out of their comfort zones and taught them endurance.

The last stop before Rishikesh was the Vashista Gufa. Here Vashishta, who was one of the seven saptarishis, had lived for several years. Subsequently, many other sages meditated here. The place was calm and had a serene atmosphere. Tara sat on the floor and meditated for some time. It was really quiet and peaceful. She was hesitant to leave. The trip was ending and everyone was a little sad. Jaya and Tara thanked Keerti Singh and gave him big tips. But it was clear that Keerti Singh's role in this yatra was beyond thanks. Like nature, he had been extra kind to the two friends in the entire trip. Keerti Singh plucked a lot of Himalayan curry leaves for Jaya. Jaya would take it back home and make chutney with it.

They arrived at Parmarth Niketan Ashram late in the evening and attended the evening Ganga arti. Swami Chidanand Saraswati and Sadhvi Bhagawati Saraswati were traveling and they were not present at the arti. The energy was not the same and Tara realized how much of a difference some people could make. When the Swami was at the Parmarth Ashram, dignitaries from all over the world visited him and attended the arti. Everything was a notch more glorious. However the sunset over the Ganges was beautiful as ever. Jaya and Tara sat at the banks of the Ganges for a long time before going for dinner. They were sad to bid goodbye to the Ganges. The course was over and the canteen was closed. So they ate dinner at Chotiwala which was a well known restaurant in Rishikesh.

Early next morning, Tara left for the Dehradun airport. She made a pact with Jaya to go to Kailash in two years. Tara was headed to Mumbai and had planned a trip to Kolhapur with school friends. Jaya was headed to Hyderabad to meet her Guru. But they met sooner than planned. Jaya's flight got rescheduled and they met at the Delhi airport for lunch. It felt like the Chardham trip extended for another meal. Soon the two friends parted and went separate ways. The great Himalayan trip was over.

CHAPTER 17

Talacauvery

Soon after the Chardham trip, Tara turned fifty. She had planned to go to Tekkady in Kerala and spend her birthday in the forests. Tara had never seen Indian wild elephants and it was her long time desire to see one. If she got lucky, she would see one in Tekkady. Tekkady was home to plenty of other wild animals and birds too. Moreover, the source of the Periyar river, which was an important component in St. Thomas's travels in India, was also located in these forests. Tara could not think of a better way to celebrate her fiftieth birthday. However, that year the Periyar river flooded and brought about a catastrophe in Kerala. Rivers were like that. Once in a while, it becomes an instrument of colossal death and destruction. Traveling to Kerala was impossible.

So when her birthday arrived, Tara found herself headed to Mookambika temple in Kollur. This temple was famous for the ritual of Vidyarambam, in which children learned to write for the first time. Tara, mainly, chose to go to Kollur because Shankaracharya had also spend some time at this place, meditating. Once again, like in Kalady, Tara found her plans changing, in such a way, that it brought Shankaracharya in focus.

It was a long drive to Kollur, through lush forests, more than a hundred kilometers away from Mangalore. Kollur was one among the seven most holiest pilgrimage sites in

Karnataka. The temple's architecture was simple like the Kerala temples. In fact, people from Kerala patronized this temple in large numbers. The temple had good energy and Tara was happy she came here on her birthday.

After darshan, Tara closed her eyes and meditated at the spot called Sankara Simhasanam, which was the exact spot Shankaracharya sat in meditation, hundreds of years ago. When she opened her eyes, she saw some pigeons pecking away at some grains on the floor, next to her. Only a few days ago, residents of her building, proposed placing nets to discourage pigeons from visiting. They were annoyed at the filth the pigeons brought with them. Tara had witnessed pigeons getting seriously injured, by getting caught in nets. She had strongly opposed the nets. Tara also continued feeding any pigeon who visited her window. A flock of pigeons always hung around her kitchen window. They would flutter around every time they saw her. In Kollur, it appeared as though the pigeons were thanking Tara because she stood up for their kind. Tara thought it was a message from the divine.

Tara had left home at five in the morning without eating anything. Before leaving the temple, she ate a simple but satisfying breakfast of idlis and vadas. It was a birthday well spend. After the Chardham trip, there was a lull in Tara's spiritual activity. She knew that there was more work to do. Perhaps, Kailash will bring more clarity. But the pre Chardham excitement was missing. Tara meditated regularly and to everyone around her, appeared more peaceful. The questions about Moksha and God remained, but the urgency to find answers was not there.

For some reason, Tara went in to a phase of deep cleaning of house for a couple of months. It felt as though she was clearing up clutter from her mind and life. She was also savoring her past. In the middle of her cleaning, her attention fell on the book "The Teaching of the Bhagavad Gita by Dayanada Swami." This was the book Jai had gifted her on the banks of Ganga in Rishikesh. She posted a picture of the book in her school group saying that one day she would read the book. Jai asked her to start right away.

"Why not" said Tara and she started to read the book. Once she began, Tara could not keep the book down. The book kept her captivated till the last page. It was as though all her muddled thoughts about God was untangled and neatly summarized in the book. The book said that the sum total of everything was God. God was like the ocean and we were like waves of the ocean. The waves of the ocean came from the ocean, it was the ocean, and it will return to the ocean. This reminded Tara of the 13th century Persian Poet Rumi's quote "You are not a drop in the ocean, you are the ocean in a drop."

Tara had for a long time now, known that she was connected to the universe. Her very existence of body and mind was possible because of a constant exchange of matter and ideas. One connected conscience whole as God made a lot of sense to her. Moreover, it did not contradict any beliefs she already had. Every religion talked about the omnipotence of God. God was everywhere and knew everything. The book said that, only way this was possible, was if God was everything.

Moreover, the Gita emphasized that the management of likes and dislikes was necessary to gain Moksha. This was Vipassana all over for Tara. She was thrilled and surprised by the content of the Gita. It was more philosophy than religion. Though she lived in India for so long, she had no idea about the nature of the Gita. This reading was a revelation. Tara felt it would have been a great personal loss if she had not read the Gita in her lifetime. Though, the book, "The Teaching of the Bhagavad Gita", was only an introduction to Gita, Tara knew she had seen enough to understand its merits. Now that Tara had a definition of God she was happy with, she spend more and more time in nature. Everything was God, but God was surely at his best in nature.

Though they had planned to meet only after two years, Jaya decided to spend new years eve with Tara in Mangalore. Jaya always meant spiritual progress for Tara. In the spirit of Chardham, Tara decided to take Jaya to Talacauvery, which was the source of the Cauvery river. Cauvery was one of the seven holy rivers in Hinduism. Talacauvery was located in Brahmagiri hills in the Coorg district. The two friends drove to Brahmagiri which was about a hundred and fifty kilometers away from Mangalore. They went through lush forests and small villages. People were very friendly and helpful because two women were traveling alone. They chose a circular route wherein they went to Talacauvery via Kerala and returned to Mangalore staying within Karnataka. It was a beautiful drive.

They stayed at Cauvery resorts which was a resort spread over fifty acres of agricultural land near Talacauvery. The owner of the resort told them that if you strike anywhere on the ground there would be Cauvery water. The hills were filled with water. The Cauvery river flows underground in Brahmagiri and resurfaces only at Bhagamandala. Only the source of the river was visible and was inside a temple pond. Tara and Jaya decided to take a dip there, the very same evening, they reached Brahmagiri. They rushed to the temple as soon as they checked in at the resort. However, the pond was closed that evening. They had to return the next day for the traditional dip. Tara and Jaya ate dinner at a local restaurant but the food was nothing to write about. Good food was not easy to find in this trip. At night, as they sat by a campfire, Jaya talked about the fire rituals coducted by her family Guru. The Chardham yatra was mainly about the water and earth elements. The fire element needed to be explored. Tara watched the smoke and sparks of the campfire for a long time, even after Jaya went to sleep. Yes, the fire was indeed mysterious.

That day Jaya and Tara were the only guests at the resort. Next day, Tara woke up to a big crowd who had arrived late at night. They brought utensils and ingredients to cook for the group. Tara and Jaya got some free breakfast and coffee.

After breakfast, Tara headed to the temple again, to take her Cauvery dip. It was invigorating like the Ganges dip at Varanasi. The water at the source had a peculiar energy. Tara felt really blessed.

When they returned to the resort, Tara decided to get some free lunch from the group. Feeding two people would be easy for a group of about hundred people. Moreover, the restaurants looked unappealing. Jaya was embarrassed and gave the head of the group a lot of money to use as donations in their temple trips. The group had a big itinerary planned of spiritual places to visit.

"We can never always compensate for all we receive, right away. We eat here free and we feed someone else free some other time" said Tara.

"That is true" agreed Jaya.

Jaya and Tara returned to Mangalore late at night. Tara was tired from the long drive and had a slight headache. She was not sure she could cook dinner. May be they would get dinner delivered home. She rested for a while and felt better. She decided she could make dinner after all. She made some clear soup and mooli parathas. It was really worth the effort. After the food they had on the trip, a home cooked meal was heaven sent. The last dinner of 2018 was simply awesome for the two exhausted friends. The year 2018, the year of their Chardham yatra, would always remain special for Tara and Jaya.

CHAPTER 18

Ganga Sagar

Tara decided to travel more for spiritual progress. Nirvana was evasive and she would not mind attaining it. She was ready to continue to make some efforts towards it. Tara did not know anyone who knew what Nirvana was. It was unexplored territory and Tara followed her own whims in chasing Nirvana. Ancient Indians loved chasing rivers and Tara inherited some of that love.

Tara decided to go to Gangasagar which was the place where a branch of the river Ganges met the sea. Moreover, Gangasagar was near Kolkata, a city Tara had wanted to visit forever. Tara was fascinated by the Bengali culture. The literature of Tagore and the movies of Satyajit Ray had build beautiful images of West Bengal in her mind. Tara had always loved the food and fashion of Kolkata but now she found out the Ganges connection.

The Ganges enters West Bengal and divides into two branches known as Padma and Bhagirathi in Murshidabad district. The Padma river enters Bangladesh while the Bhagirathi river flows through West Bengal. The other names of the Bhagirathi river are Kat Ganga and Hooghly. Ganga loses her identity in Murshidabad. It is the Hooghly river which joins the Bay of Bengal at Gangasagar. The Padma river would join the Bay of Bengal a little further in Bangladesh. Kolkata was a city on the banks of the Hooghly river, in all her glory, ready to meet the sea. It was this reason, above all others, that made Tara really thrilled about her trip to Kolkata.

Tara lived in Mangalore and connectivity was a problem. Often, there was an intermediate bigger airport before any destination. This time there was a long layover at Chennai airport. A journey that began at seven in the morning at Mangalore concluded around five in the evening at Kolkata airport. Tara took an Ola cab to the Hotel Treebo which was near a police station. It was an unfamiliar city and Tara was traveling alone. The police station was the reason, she chose the hotel, because it made her feel more secure. Hussein, the Ola cab driver, who dropped her to the hotel, became her guide and driver for the rest of her stay in Kolkata, all the way, to the airport drop back. Tara had enquired about a good tour guide during the cab ride, casually, and Hussein had volunteered to become her guide. It was as easy as that. Tara realized that she was never alone. Everywhere there were people to help and guide her. Security was not in police stations but in the goodness that exist in the people she met.

Tara tried to eat a real Bengali meal the very evening she reached Kolkata. She had researched all the good restaurants in Kolkata and she chose to go to a restaurant called "Bojohari Manna" that evening. The Treebo hotel staff arranged a Uber driver who dropped her at a mall. She could not find the restaurant, anywhere, in the mall. Tara, then, waved in a taxi, and used the Google map to find Bojohari Manna. But the place was closed. It was getting late, and all the food joints appeared closed. It was Tara's first evening in Kolkata and she was getting a little worried. But Kolkata appeared safe because young women were walking, leisurely, on the streets at that hour. Moreover, the taxi driver stayed with her and dropped her to another restaurant called "Ghare bahare". It was worth all the trouble. It turned out to be the place for the best Bengali food in Kolkata. She tasted Bengali Moong dal, Mustard fish curry, and Mishti doi for the first time. For once, Tara wished she had the ability to eat more. She could not finish the big, delicious, thali the restaurant served. Yes, Kolkata food was simply amazing. Tara had tried her hand at Bengali cooking without ever tasting an authentic Bengali meal. She was pleasantly surprised that she had managed to get the Bengali cuisine, right, all along. Tara returned to her room a little later than, what she would, typically, do in a strange city. But she was one happy woman and looked forward to the next morning.

Hussein arrived early morning to take Tara to Gangasagar. Hussein had an old car in which all the viewing mirrors were missing. Tara was a little worried about her safety but Hussein turned out to be a good driver. He sped through the roads overtaking almost every vehicle. He popped his head out of the car windows, every time, he had to judge road traffic. It appeared as though Hussein was born with a steering wheel in his hand. Tara knew she was in good hands and quickly stopped worrying about his unconventional driving practices.

The trip to Gangasagar was through rural areas where time appeared to have stood still. These villages might have looked the same thousands of years back. Compared to South Indian villages, development in West Bengal villages were slow. There were no cars or televisions in most houses. The houses were made of natural materials like wood and grass. There were paddy farms all along the road. Most houses were surrounded by ponds and Tara saw women catching fish from the ponds with nets. Large houses where big joined families lived were hidden behind simple entrances. Everyone was busy tending to home and farm. People took good care of each other.

In some places, an entire village was inhabited by members of the same family. There was a community kitchen where meals were cooked for the entire village. Tara really loved the idea of a community kitchen. She was witnessing how hard it was for senior citizens to provide healthy meals for themselves. Most of the times, they depend on paid househelp for their meals, which meant, changing of lifelong diet habits. Here, the aged could eat what they ate all their lives and they were not a burden on anyone's time. It was a refreshing change from the rest of India, where more and more aged people lived alone, because their children had migrated to other countries for more wealth generation. Tara thought lack of wealth and development was a blessing in disguise for these villages. They could focus on what was really important. Tara was sure that any development that would come in the future should try hard to preserve these values.

Hussein parked his car at Kakdwip and accompanied Tara by ferry to Sagar islands. Tara had to cross the Hooghly river to get to Sagar islands. The Ganges is never small. She is always huge. But here, as Hooghly, she was simply magnificent. It was not clear whether she became the sea or the sea became her. Moreover, the Hooghly river was the smaller of the two branches of the Ganges. The river Padma which would flow mostly in Bangladesh was much larger. For once, Tara felt sorry that the British had divided Bangladesh from India. In the process, they had torn a part of Gangaji from India. To follow the Padma river, Tara would require a visa.

Seagulls followed Tara's boat, for a long time after leaving the harbor, for food. It was a crowded boat but Hussein had managed to get her a really good spot. He also gave Tara some food to feed the seagulls. The long boat ride on the Hooghly river was some kind of closure for Tara, in her chasing the Ganga story.

When they arrived at the Sagar islands, Tara tried to pay her respects to the river. While Hussein went to arrange for a rickshaw driver, Tara walked to the banks of the river. The boundaries were dirtied with human feces and Tara struggled to find a clean spot. Here, typically, like in other parts of the country, people should have done Ganga artis to the river, every morning and evening. Instead, to Tara's horror, she found it dirtied. She quickly did her pranams to the river before beginning a one hour rickshaw ride across Sagar islands to reach Gangasagar. It was a pleasant ride through timeless, ancient looking villages.

Tara was happy to see that Gangasagar was pristine and clean. The place had many shops that sold shell bangles and many other traditional artifacts. Tara bought some shell bangles for herself and Jaya. She remembered that Jaya loved shell bangles too. And then she went on to take her dips in the ocean. A priest gave her some flowers and food to offer to the ocean and chanted some mantras for a fee. The Gangasagar water was refreshing and not too salty because here the river was more dominant than the ocean. They say every river joins the sea to become the ocean. At Gangasagar, this becoming was even more obvious. Tara would have loved to stay, all afternoon, in the water like a kid. She hated to leave the place.

Before leaving, Tara paid her respects at the Kapil muni temple. Hussein found a small local restaurant where they ate a delicious lunch thali with Rahu fish fry. They took a completely different, but equally beautiful route, that involved ferry and rickshaw rides, back to where their car was parked. The journey became even more pleasant as the sun set. Hussein joined Tara for dinner at 6 Ballygunge place which was one of the famous restaurants of Kolkata. Tara tried dal with fish head for the first time and it was delicious. Tara had tried cooking with fish heads before and she was not a big fan of it. But the Bengalis knew how to use fish heads and even fish bones to make delicious dishes. Tara also loved the patrani machi which was fish steamed in banana leaves. Tara could not get over how delicious, food continued to be in Kolkata.

The next day would be reserved for exploring the city. Kolkata is named after Kalikata devi of Kalighat Temple. Tara decided to go to the Kalighat temple, first thing, in the morning. Hibiscus flowers are very popular flowers of worship in West Bengal and they formed a sea of red at the entrance of temples. Tara bought some puja offerings and was accompanied by a priest while entering the temple. One senior priest caught hold of her and asked her if she had any kids. When she said no, he started performing rites for an offspring without asking her permission. He also charged a lot of money for the pooja she did not want to perform. When she was free of him, all the money in her purse was gone. It was known that wishes came true by visiting this temple. Tara did not care for an offspring but there was a small wart on her finger that was bothering her for a year. She prayed for it to be gone and it was gone in two days. It was like a miracle. The Kalighat temple indeed was powerful. No wonder so many people came here for worship from all over the world.

Kolkata was the city where Mother Teresa, who was the epitome of compassion and love, did most of her charity work. Tara saw the building where Mother Teresa lived and died. She also visited Mother Teresa's tomb and spend some time in the premises. It was a serene place and Tara could feel the presence of Mother Teresa from beyond her grave. Tara got goosebumps as she knelt and prayed near the tomb. In that moment, she felt truly blessed.

Next, Tara visited the Victoria memorial which was an imposing structure that served as an example of brilliant British architecture. The memorial had splendid museums and gardens. However, there were no memories preserved of British days in India. The memorial served only as an imposing shell of history. On the contrary, the bed and rooms of Netaji Subash Chandra Bose's house, which was Tara's next stop, looked as though they were awaiting his return. Netaji had gone missing in Japan, during the second world war. The route Netaji used to escape when the British police came to arrest him was marked for everyone to see. After her stop at Netaji's house, Tara visited Rabindranath Tagore's house. The house was in the middle of a busy road. It was huge and build for comfort. Tagore belonged to the rich Zamindar class of India. His poetry and writings were displayed in all the rooms. Unlike imposing memorials, the homes of Netaji and Tagore were sanctified by memories.

There were a lot of marble art shops near Tagore's house. Art was everywhere in Kolkata. Tara's next stop was Kumortuli, which was where the potters lived in Kolkata. Huge clay statues of goddesses were in all stages of making. Tara bought a small Kali ma statue to take back home.

Then Tara proceeded to Dakshineshwar Kali ma temple who was the Deity of Vivekananda's guru, Ramakrishna

Paramahamsa. From there she took a boat ride to Belur Mutt, which was an organization of Vivekananda. It brought back memories of Vivekananda Ashram in Kanyakumari. It was getting late in the evening and Tara did not have much time to spend here. The loud chirping of birds told her it was definitely a great place to spend some serious time. On her way back, Tara watched the Ganga arti from the boat, all along the Hooghly river. She also got to cross the Howrah bridge which was made famous in Hindi movies. No visit to Calcutta is considered complete without visiting this bridge.

Tara expressed her desire to pay respects to the Hooghly river. Hussein took her to a ghat from where the river was accessible. The ghats were filled with slush and was slippery. Tara lost her grip and almost fell in to the river. Hussein was watching from afar. He yelled at her to remove her slippers. Tara then found it easier to maneuver bare feet. It was good to touch the Ganges water one last time. Ganga would always have a special place in her heart.

Hussein had watched over her like a parent, making sure she was safe. Tara had given him a long list of places she wanted to visit when she first arrived. Hussein made sure every place was covered. Even after Tara was ready to call it a day and return to the hotel, Hussein took her to Eden gardens, where international cricket happens, because it was on her list. Tara only saw it from outside. It was getting late and it was time for dinner. She had seen so much of Kolkata in one day. She was satisfied and grateful to Hussein. Like Keerti Singh in Chardham and the unknown horse rider in Kedarnath, Hussein was an important component in the success of the Kolkata visit.

Finally, Tara found an open Bojohari manna restaurant, where they stopped for the last dinner of the trip. Tara tried steamed Hilsa in mustard sauce and Giant shrimp in tender coconut. They were also served Mishti doi and many other delicacies. Needless to say, it was another of Kolkata's delicious lavish meals which was impossible to finish.

Back home, Tara relished the prasad she brought back from the Kalighat temple wrapped in some kind of fragrant leaves. It was another reminder of the exquisite cuisine of Kolkata. Kolkata had given her much in terms of history and culture. Time and again, Tara wondered about the miracle at Kalighat temple. Why would God who was the sum of all things answer prayers? The question left her intrigued.

CHAPTER 19

Dharamshala

It was time to progress in Vipassana and take another ten day course. From now on, Tara planned to attend Vipassana courses across India instead of going back to Kerala, again. Thus, she could combine her love for travel with spiritual progress. She decided to go to Dharamshala in Himachal Pradesh, which was the home of Dalai Lama and many Tibetans in exile. Moreover, Dharamshala was located in the Himalayas. Hence, Tara had no second thoughts about choosing the center. It was an overnight journey from Mangalore to Gaggal with two intermediate stops at Bangalore and Delhi airports. The early morning car ride from the Gaggal airport to the Vipassana center at Dharamkot was surreal. The roads were lined with pine trees and the weather was cheerful and warm.

The Dharamkot Vipassana center was situated on a hill and there was a slight climb to Tara's room. The fragrance of pine trees filled the air. The view of the Himalayas from the center was enchanting. There were many monkey families living in the vicinity of the center. The students were advised to neither feed the monkeys nor make any gestures towards them, including eye contacts. All the paths in the center were covered with metal cages for protection. This was one of the few times Tara had witnessed people enclosing themselves in cages, so that animals could live freely outside. Vipassana centers followed a principle of nonviolence towards all, including animals.

Soon the course officially began, and Tara handed over her mobile phones and valuables to the center, before entering in to silence for ten days. Like the Vipassana courses she attended in Kerala, each day, the meditation sessions lasted from Four Thirty in the morning to Nine in the night. Since she was a senior student, her last meal for the day would be at Twelve noon. However, at Dharamshala, it was mandatory for senior students to leave the meditation hall, whenever the teachers talked to the new students. Tara was worried she would sleep off in her room, so she decided to meditate outside in nature. But the teacher insisted that the rule was that the students need to stay in their designated rooms. Thus, in Dharamshala, Tara found herself meditating for a couple of hours, each day, inside her own room.

Everyone, typically, sat on the floor to meditate. Tara had struggled with sitting on the floor and kept shifting her legs, every ten minutes, through all her Vipassana courses. There were sessions where students have to commit to sit still for one hour. For Tara, those sessions were impossible, sitting on the floor, and had to resort to using a chair. She had observed other students using pillows to make themselves comfortable. But pillows had not proved particularly useful for Tara, so far. Alone, in her room, Tara decided to try using pillows one more time and she finally learned the trick. The idea was to use pillows to stuff all the areas between her comfortable folded legs position and the floor. There were no restrictions on the number or type of pillows. It was all about finding that comfortable zone. It was an Eureka moment. Finally, in the third Vipassana course, Tara could sit calmly on the floor and meditate like all the other students.

Tara attained bhang, again, and felt peaceful, perhaps a little more intensely than in her previous courses. At the end of ten days, Tara knew she had to work harder and do more courses before she fully understood the Vipassana technique. For now she was content. Tara was sad to the leave the center, nestled in the laps of the Himalayas, which was her home for a short while. She was glad she chose to stay back for a couple more days to explore Dharamshala.

Tara decided to stay at Unmad, which was a hotel, run by a group of three young friends, who came from the advertising world. They pursued art, writing, and hiking, along with doing all the cooking, cleaning, and managing for the guests. They considered running Unmad as Karma Yoga, which meant service without expectations. They had given up high paying jobs in Delhi to run Unmad and now lived a more contend life. Aparna and Rahul were present at Unmad to receive Tara. It was a bit of a climb to Tara's room at Unmad and Tara never traveled light. She got help with her luggage from Suman, the cab driver, who dropped her at Unmad from the Vipassana center. He also became her guide for the rest of her stay in Dharamshala. Cab drivers, often, doubled as tour guides in Dharamshala. Tourism was one of the main sources of income in Dharamshala.

As soon as the checkin at Unmad was over, Tara was ready to explore McLeod Ganj, where the Tibetan community in exile had settled. After a brief stop at the Buddha temple, Tara visited the Dalai Lama temple, which was also the residence of the current Dalai Lama. To Tara's disappointment, the Dalai Lama was not in town when she visited. After that she spend some time at the Norbulingka Institute where she saw many Tibetan artisans at work. Each room of the institute was filled with painters, weavers, carpenters, and other artists. Tara also stopped at Gyuto Tantric Monastery, which was where many Tibetan monks lived.

Everything about the Tibetan people was peaceful. Their temples and streets were splendid and colorful. The huge rotating prayer wheels and the colossal golden statues of Buddha gave testament to the glory of Tibet's ancient culture. Even in exile, it was evident that Tibetans had always known only abundance. They knew how to thrive in the cold snow covered Himalayas. They knew how to create abundance wherever they went. However, Tara could not help wishing the return of Dalai Lama to Tibet. The aged monks she saw in Dharamshala looked sad and may have lost all hope of ever returning home. China made a lot of money by occupying Tibet. But the world, including China, was losing things way more valuable than money by destroying Tibetan culture. Some day, China would do the decent thing with regards to the Dalai Lama and his people. Tara only wished it would not be too late. But the Dalai Lama was definitely good for India. The Tibetan presence in Dharamshala filled the entire region with good energy. Tara also ended her exploration of Tibet in exile on a happy note, eating momos and buying colorful shawls and jewelry.

Suman drove Tara to other places of interest in Dharamshala. The car drove along narrow mountain roads and scenic routes. Rare Himalayan butterflies and birds, which Tara had only seen in books, actually appeared along the road. Tara saw a man selling a truck load of Himalayan rock salt at Forty Rupees a kilo. Tara had never seen so much Himalayan salt before. Suman also took Tara to a tea garden which was owned privately but was accessible to public for free. Tara had never seen a tea garden though she had seen plenty of coffee plantations. Acres and acres of tea leaves met her eyes. There was definitely something about tea plantations that appealed to all, because people visited the gardens in large numbers. Moreover, Tea was Tara's favorite beverage.

After the tea gardens, Tara headed to Dal lake but it was foggy when they arrived at the place and could not even see the lake. Therefore, they did not stop at the lake and continued driving uphill to the Sahaj yoga center. Suman said that the lake was holy and it must not be missed. Tara decided that the best thing to do, perhaps, was to return the next day. After a brief visit at Sahaj yoga center, Tara and Suman had tea at sunset point. Sunset point was foggy too, but the fresh ginger tea made by a road side vendor was good. On the way back, they again arrived at Dal lake. This time the fog had lifted and Tara could see the lake clearly. It was beautiful and full of fish.

She also paid her respects at the temple at Dal lake. As her car was leaving the Dal lake area, the fog came back and the lake was barely visible. Nature was once again kind to Tara. Her visit to Dal lake had gone well. The last stop for the day was at the Church of St. John in the wilderness. True to it's name, it was a beautiful church in the middle of a jungle. The Church cemetery contained the grave of Lord Elgin who served as the Governor General of India during British rule. The place was serene and perfect for a final resting place.

Tara reminisced about the eventful day as she watched the sunset from Unmad. She had done a lot in one day. Aparna and Rahul cooked her a dinner of Chilli Paneer and also entertained her with excellent conversations. Tara marveled at how much these two young people had to say and offer to each guest who arrived at Unmad.

The next day was reserved to get to know the people of Dharamshala, a little more closely. Suman first showed Tara his house and hotel rooms owned by his family. Some parts of his house had traditional roofs made of stone tiles. Concrete roofs were now more common. Stone tiles were a rare sight which would soon disappear unless someone thought of preserving tradition. Stone tiles had protected village houses from landslides in the past. Tara was surprised that Suman's family owned so much property. Suman was an MBA graduate who was writing entrance exams required for Government jobs. Suman was from a tribal community though Tara could not tell from his modern attire. Suman explained that tribal attires were donned only during festivals and weddings. Himachal Pradesh was also called Devabhoomi like Uttrakhand, but the population of Himachal Pradesh was mainly tribal and hence their religious rituals revolved around nature more than temples.

The most popular temples were Snake temples in Himachal Pradesh. Thus, the first destination for the day was the ancient Bhagsunag temple. This temple was dedicated to a Nag who defeated the demon Bhagsu who stole water. After paying her respects at the temple, Tara spend some time at the Bhagsu waterfall which was in the vicinity of the temple. After that, Tara headed to Kareri village where Suman arranged for a home cooked lunch at his friend's house. The trip to Kareri village provided beautiful breathtaking views. Curry leaves grew all along the road and Tara was reminded of the Chardham yatra. Moreover, the village visit demonstrated to Tara that the people of the region lived a simple life of sufficiency. They were not extremely wealthy but there was no scarcity either. The lunch was a simple meal of rice, roti, kadi, and pickle made on a firewood stove.

It was really delicious but they would not accept money for it. Following Suman's advice, Tara quietly handed some money to a child. The women of Himachal Pradesh were strikingly beautiful and hardworking. Only the fit could survive these cold mountains. Most activity involved steep climbing along rough paths.

On the way back to Dharamshala from Kareri village they briefly stopped at Indrunag temple on the top of a hill. This snake god was responsible for protecting the population from heavy rain fall and bad weather. That would be the last stop of the trip. Tara had traveled to Dharamshala in August in the peak of the monsoon season. All rains happened while she was indoors at the Vipassana center. And there was a brief rain when she was in the car and returning from Kareri village. All other times it had been bright and sunny. To top it all, she also saw a beautiful rainbow from the Unmad balcony on her last evening at Dharamshala. She definitely had the blessings of Indrunag on this trip. Moreover, since tourism was slow during the monsoon, they were also spared the frequent traffic blocks that occur when tourism was at its peak season.

The next morning Suman dropped Tara to the airport. On the way he showed her the library where youngsters like Suman spend all the time studying for entrance exams. After dropping her, he was planning to go back to the library. Tara wished him luck before parting. The youth of India was India's greatest asset. There was no stopping them. They were well mannered, responsible, hardworking, and not afraid of dreaming big.

Tara's flight which was supposed to be at Seven in the morning was delayed till Four in the evening. But she had no complaints. She was happy to linger at the Dharamshala airport from where she could see the Himalayas. There was something comforting to be in the proximity of the Himalayas. Back home, after her third course, Tara could do Vipassana meditation on her own. She had finally outgrown Guru assisted meditation sessions. Over time, Tara got more and more comfortable sitting on the floor, and soon pillows were not needed, either.

CHAPTER 20

Mangalore

It was the year 2020. This was the year Tara had planned to go to Kailash. She had already paid an advance amount to a travel agent in Nepal. She also planned to go to Punjab for her Vipassana meditation course. But all travel plans came to a void in 2020. It was the year of the Corona virus and Government imposed lock downs. Traveling was impossible when even stepping out of your own house was not allowed by law. Mangalore stayed humane and sane through the epidemic compared to other cities in the country. There was panic around the globe and people forgot manners when they dealt with families in quarantine. Arjun was back in Mangalore and Tara was glad that they would survive the Corona era together.

After a few months of barely stepping out of the house, except for necessities, Tara decided to explore Mangalore with Arjun, once again. When they had first come to live in Mangalore, they had visited most of the points of interest in Mangalore and her vicinity. Once they set up home and settled down, they stopped going around Mangalore. All travel plans involved going out of Mangalore to far away places. But because of Corona, Tara had to look locally for entertainment. Like meditation, the travel within was full of pleasant surprises.

Mangalore was located at the confluence of a river and an ocean and hence was an ancient city with an important port. Ports were an important factor in the formation of ancient cities because of trade. Mangalore was a small city of temples and beaches filled with coconut trees as far as eyes could see. Mangalore was a part of the Dakshina Kannada district in Karnataka. It is said that this district has never known hunger because of the blessings of Goddess Annapoorna, who is the goddess of food and nourishment. There are only a few temples dedicated to Annapoorneshwari in India, and one of them is in Horanadu near Mangalore. It was a beautiful temple with friendly priests and an holy elephant. It was very organized and had clear instructions posted on the walls. It is said that if you do annadana in this temple you will never go hungry in your life. When Tara and Arjun visited the temple, they made an offering of rice and flowers. They also ate a simple but delicious lunch of rice, sambhar, and payasam. This meal was available free to every visitor who came to the temple. Many temples in Dakshina Kannada gave free meals to visitors. The temple in Dharamshala gave free meals to thousands of devotees everyday. As a result, there were no beggars in the district.

Mangalore was named after the Goddess Mangala devi, who was the deity held responsible for the prosperity of the city. The Mangala devi temple was situated prominently in the middle of the city and was a favorite stop for Tara and Arjun on many evenings. The main attractions at the temple were the silver idol of the goddess and the large Pipal tree which was dedicated to Nag worship. It is also believed that the temple was build to commemorate a princess from Kerala who had settled in Mangalore.

Mangalore was unpretentious and a family oriented town. The city did not do anything to attract tourists and perhaps was even a little afraid of outsiders. There were many eminent personalities with roots in Dakshina Kannada. Uncle Pai who was the creator of the comic series, Amar Chitra Katha, and movie actors like Aishwariya Rai, Shilpa Shetty, and Deepika Padukone came from this region. Many banks originated from Mangalore. The people of Mangalore went about their work meticulously and were a content lot. Karnataka was a big state that typically kept a low profile, avoiding trouble, and promoting self growth.

It was a strange twist of fate that had brought Tara to Mangalore. Half an hour away from Mangalore was her beloved ancestral state of Kerala. Yet, Tara had decided to set her roots in Mangalore. Tara had, for a long time, wanted to buy a home in India. Casual visitors to India noticed how peaceful they felt in India. Tara had always been sure that her final resting place would be India but she had not found a suitable place to settle. When Tara's dad was hospitalized, she spend a couple of weeks in Mangalore. One evening Tara's cousin Liza drove her to Infant Jesus church in Beekarnakatte to pray for her father's fast recovery. The car went through small roads along beaches and coconut tree lined roads. The Infant Jesus church campus was huge, placed on a hill, from where Tara could see almost all of Mangalore. As she watched the sunset that evening, from the church, Tara had decided to buy a home in Mangalore.

Surprisingly, after her travels, the temples of Dakshina Kannada became more interesting. The first time she visited the Krishna temple in Udupi, she had only noticed the elephant who would bless people with his trunk for a small fee. She now saw faith of the people. There were groups of women sitting around the premises singing bhajans. The Hare Rama Hare Krishna group of people were singing and dancing. Dozens of priests walking about in a rush and many other such activities. And the blessing elephant was there too.

Similarly, when she visited the Mariguddi temple which was just a couple of kilometers away from her house, the faith of the local people stood out for her. It was a powerful temple where free food was distributed every Monday and Friday to anyone who wanted to eat. The rich and the poor ate there without any special treatment. Tara could see such social equality in ice cream parlors of Mangalore too, where the rich and poor sat together and ate.

Traveling in Corona times meant face masks and maintaining social distancing. Tara and Arjun decided to visit river confluences since they were chosen places by sages to meditate. They also decided to visit popular temples they had not visited so far. Every Sunday, Arjun and Tara packed a home cooked lunch and made day trips in their family car.

One of the first temples they visited, during Corona times, was the Narahari parbat Mahadeva temple. The temples of Karnataka often contained some natural curiosities. The water in the ponds of the Narahari temple was supposed to have miraculous properties. A friendly priest did an elaborate Puja for Tara and Arjun. There were many monkeys on the premises eating coconuts offered by devotees at the temple. After enjoying their packed lunch of prawn biryani, they headed back home, making a few stops to drink coconut water. They also paid a quick visit to the Infant Jesus church en route to home. Back home the fragrance of jasmine flowers and sandalwood paste, they brought back from the temple, would last for a long time.

The Karinjeshwar temple was a little far from Mangalore and it closes by noon. It took a little planning to make it to the temple on time. There were many steps to reach the main temple and it was closed by the time Tara reached the top. However, a priest came back to open the doors of the temple and Tara had a good darshan. The priests of this temple kept walking up and down the hill to cater to the demands of the devotees. Thus, the priests of the Karinjeshwar temple were particularly fit. The place was full of monkeys and one monkey tried to snatch Tara's bag. She held on to it tight and won her right to keep her bag from the monkey. They ended the visit with a lunch of curd rice, fried potatoes, and mango pickle, sitting besides a lake, within the temple.

Visiting religious places was an excuse to travel to beautiful places and get some good sun. Most of the times, they had to pass through thick jungles to reach the temples. The fresh oxygen filled jungle air was rejuvenating. Moreover the art, decor, and architecture were always stunning. Sometimes the buildings and at other times the surroundings left lasting impressions. On the way to Polali, they saw peacocks dance by the road side. They stopped at St Joseph the worker church in Vamanjoor and admired the flowers in the garden. Churches in Mangalore always had beautiful gardens. The Eight century, Sri Raja Rajeshwari temple in Polali was a collection of simple ceramic tiled traditional buildings. But all the walls of the temple was covered in gold. Tara and Arjun was just in time for Darshan. The temple closed soon after they arrived. They made it in time for darshan without fail, every time. It was difficult to judge the time it would take to reach these faraway temples. Sometimes the roads were bad and at other times the roads were hard to find.

After the temple, they visited the Baba Fakruddin Juma Masjid at Polali. Baba Fakruddin was believed to have performed many miracles and the Polali mosque was famous in the region. Tara went to the women's section and offered her prayers. After a lunch of rotis, garlic mushroom, and dill sabji and plenty of tender coconut water breaks they returned home. On the way they stopped at Sri Ananta Padmanabha Temple, which was a snake temple in Kudupu. Tara was intrigued by a huge ant hill behind snake idol. Here nature was worshiped in all forms. Thus, every Sunday Tara and Arjun saw a lot of Mangalore, closely.

Another fine Sunday, Tara and Arjun headed to Sasihitlu beach, where the rivers Pavanje and Shambhavi met the sea. The Sasihitlu temple was one of a kind and its floors were made of beach sand. Tara spend some time at the sangam of the two rivers. She could never get over the fact how the meeting of two water bodies was always so gentle. The packed lunch of chapati, cabbage, cluster beans and potato sabji, sweet mango pickle tasted delicious. Everything tasted so much better outdoors. On the way back home they stopped at the Bappa nadu temple in Mulki which was a Hindu temple believed to be build by a Muslim merchant. The final stop of the day was at St Antony's church in Kuloor. This church was on top of a hill and the view from the church was breathtaking.

On one of their Sunday trips, Tara and Arjun stopped at the Sayyid Muhammad Shareeful Madani Darga in Ullal on their way to Manjeshwar. This Darga was famous and every time someone new came to Mangalore, Tara took them here. There was a women's section at the Darga where Tara could offer her prayers. At Manjeshwar, Tara and Arjun walked on a long man made sea walk to the point where the Uppala river meets the sea. Soon afterwards, on another weekend, they visited Kodi Bengre Delta beach, where the river Suvarna met the Arabian sea.

Finally, one Sunday they went to the Ullal Endpoint estuary where the rivers Netravathi and Gurupura merges with the Arabian sea. These rivers were personal to Tara. She could see the Gurupura river from her house. She saw the Netravati river every time she visited her farm house. There were plenty of fish factories on the way to endpoint. There was some sea food drying all over the place. A place where two major rivers meet the sea is always revered in Indian culture but here the place was not given much prominence. Tara thought that there was so much scope to develop the estuary as a tourist destination.

By now, the Corona scare was subsiding and Tara and Arjun slowly started eating out at restaurants. If they were not going on long drives, they would go for long walks. The Tannirbhavi beach was very close to where they lived. They would walk to Sultan Battery and then catch a local ferry to go to the beach. On other days, they would walk to Urwa church, Mariguddi temple, or the Kudroli temple. Sometimes they would go in their scooter to the Kadri temple. There were streets in Mangalore where there were rows of temples. There were many mosques and churches worth visiting too. Many of the churches were more than a hundred years old. The ceilings and walls of the Aloysius chapel were painted, beautifully, by the Italian Jesuit, Antonio Moscheni, in 1899. This chapel is now preserved and functions as a museum. Mangalore could easily become a Pilgrimage destination but the city did not present that picture. In fact, the city did very little to promote tourism of any kind. But Mangalore, clearly, was a big factor in Tara's spiritual progress.

In the beginning of the year 2021, Tara was thanking Jai for the Bhagvad Gita introduction and asked him, jokingly, to become her Guru. To her surprise, he invited her to join the Gita classes he had been conducting for years. A lot of Tara's schoolmates also showed interest and thus began the reading of the nine volume series "The Bhagavad Gita—Home study course" by Swami Dayananda Saraswati. The course was taught online and was conducted, every evening, from Monday to Saturday. On Sundays, classes were held in the morning. The classes lasted for about two hours. If Tara was looking to understand what Moksha was, she had to look no further. Gita was known as the Moksha Shastra, the science of Moksha. In the Corona era, when everyone was feeling trapped, Tara slowly developed a sense of liberation.

When the air travel restrictions were lifted, Arjun went back to America. Tara decided to visit the Sri Ananthapadmanabha Swamy Lake Temple in Ananthapura, Kerala, on her own. The car battery had died because the car was used rarely. It was the day of the Saraswathi Pooja and so no mechanics were available. Luckily, her neighbor helped her to jump start the car. It was a bright and beautiful day and Tara's father accompanied her. A vegetarian crocodile lived in the temple lake but Tara did not get to see it. But she did get to see lotus ponds, fish, and snakes. Tara's father was rigid in his Christian faith and did not enter the temple. He waited for Tara outside the temple. But he was happy with the lunch they had at Kumbla. Food in Kerala was always delicious. On the return from Kerala, they were stopped and asked to provide covid free certification. Luckily everyone was vaccinated and they were allowed to return home. It was a reminder that Corona was not over yet. Traveling outside Karnataka might mean quarantines for days away from home. From then on, traveling lost all its charm for Tara, for a long time.

There were two kinds of people Tara encountered in Mangalore. The first kind were very chauvinistic and were offended even if Tara only opened her mouth. It was always some kind of power play with them. They acted in groups to feel better when they behaved idiotically. Tara taught Mathematics at local colleges for a couple of years and then decided to retire. It was impossible to work while facing this kind of attitude. Then there was another kind of people asking her to do more and totally got her. They were mostly young and unstoppable. Unlike academics, where only the experts could tell who was skilled, their skill was obvious to all. They were hardworking and efficient.

Though, Tara had to give up everything she was before coming to Mangalore, it was these good people who made her stay worthwhile. Her students, each one of them, had worked very hard and did as best as they could in the exams. Even after she stopped working, it always felt good to see her students. They clearly appreciated her teaching. Tara was touched seeing young people work hard. In fact, hard working people were Tara's tribe. Her building manager, Rakesh, would get her drivers, carpenters, electricians, and provide help without fail every time she needed help. He was a Management graduate and could deliver. There was a contentment in him that Tara appreciated greatly. It was just not the people of Mangalore who were contend. The animals were contend too. Even stray dogs and cats took their time before they ate anything you fed them. Avarice was not a quality of Mangaloreans. Tara's housekeepers, apart from keeping her house clean, could get her any plants or goods she desired. They knew where to get it from. The people on Mangalore roads were very encouraging towards women drivers. They were very patient with mistakes made by beginners. A lot of industry in Mangalore were conducted by women which was proof of existence of men who were not chauvinistic. Even the chauvinistic men left Tara alone as long as she kept away.

There were many other reasons like the best hospitals and police in the country to stay in Mangalore. But the most important of them all was her parents. They now lived next door. Tara had often craved their company after she left home. Now they were near her all the time. It was their sunset years and it made her heart happy to see them. Thus, Tara spend her days in Mangalore, blissfully, watching the ocean, the Gurupura river, and the rising and setting of the sun from her balcony.

CHAPTER 21

Charmadi

The Charmadi farm was love at first sight for Tara. Her Uncle, she fondly called Papichi, owned the farm. The two acres farm was in a village called Kolumbe, on the banks of the Netravati river, surrounded by paddy farms. The primary crop of the farm was coconuts and Tara could not ask for more. If there was a farm of her dreams, then this would be it. Thus, when Papichi decided to sell the farm, Tara decided to buy it from him.

At Charmadi, the river Netravati was still young and close to it's source. For most of the year, it looked like a gentle stream. In the monsoons, the water levels would rise and submerge a bridge connecting the two different shores of the river. Thus, this bridge needed to be build, every year, by the local people. However, in the year 2019, the river flooded, resulting in the evacuation of the entire Kolumbe village for a couple of days, accompanied with major property destruction. Two years since the floods, Tara was the first person to buy property in the Kolumbe village. The floods had scared potential buyers for a long time. For Tara, everything about a river was sacred even the floods. It was in the nature of the gentlest rivers to rage, at least once in hundred years, and bring about considerable destruction. You could live alongside a river, only if you are willing to bear the brunt of it's moods.

It was the December of 2021 and Corona was still a looming threat. Tara had hardly left home and so had never taken a PCR test. But even to enter the land registration office, everyone had to test for Corona. Thus, Tara did her first nose swab test the day she registered her Charmadi property. The test was a little unpleasant but not painful. She was relieved when the test results came out negative, otherwise it meant quarantine for fourteen days. Tara was more afraid of the quarantine than the disease because Corona had become less deadly by now. Most people who were afflicted by it were recovering well.

After registration, Papichi visited the farm and explained all the work he had done to Tara. It was for the first time she looked closely at the work he was doing. Farm visits usually meant eating delicious food and enjoying nature, so far. Now she saw all the hard work. She gained a new respect for her extended family who were mostly land owners. No one taught agriculture in schools. Knowledge was passed on by word of mouth. You had to be in the field to learn. Tara's family knew all about farming. Many of her uncles had traveled to remote places and converted useless mountain lands in to profitable rubber plantations. Their arrival would usher in prosperity for entire villages. Finally, Tara was entering the profession of her ancestors. She was sad to see Papichi drive away. Tara knew that Papichi was selling simply because he had aged and could not manage the farm anymore. His children were urbanized and were not interested in maintaining a farm. The changes that came with aging relatives were always painful. She only hoped she could do justice to the farm for the sake of Papichi.

Papichi introduced Tara to Monappan who had been the caretaker of the property for many years. He let Tara decide whether she wanted to retain Monappan's service. There was a small storage building in the property. To test Monappan, Tara asked him to tidy up the place before her next visit. After a week, when Tara visited Charmadi, the building and it's vicinity including a defunct well and an abandoned toilet were all cleaned up. Monappan was definitely a one man army. Tara knew he was a good find and he was hired as the caretaker, from then on. Monappan's sister Chinnamma agreed to be her housekeeper.

Tara was lucky to find help because Labor had become sparse in rural areas. All the young people had moved away to big cities or to other countries. India had been an agrarian society from ancient times but now agriculture was a dying profession. Young people were disenchanted with farming. The Indian Government over the years made sure everyone became literate by going to school. However, traditional skills were not taught in schools but learned at home from family. In fact, most jobs you could get by going to school were service jobs for which one had to migrate. Farming was not a job preferred by the educated young. They would rather become laborers and drivers in far off places. Their lives did not, necessarily, get better by these choices they made. They could not deal with the stress of leaving their rural homes which were cradles of love and affection. Mass migrations were changing family and economic dynamics all over India. The villages were filled with aged people struggling to perform their daily chores. Everyone was asking Tara to invest in more land but she knew it was a bad idea looking at the labor situation.

Tara needed a place to stay while she developed the farm since it was Eighty Kilometers away from Mangalore. She decided to convert the existing storage building in to a temporary home. Her cousin Sanoj took on the job of refurbishing the building. Tara had always wanted to live in a traditional house with mud walls and ceramic roof tiles. But when they inspected the existing mud walls of the storage building, it was full of termite colonies. Therefore, all the mud walls of the old building were torn down and it was decided to construct only brick walls. Moreover, it was not possible to find people who would build with mud. Mud construction was out of fashion. Everyone build with concrete because it was durable. However, concrete houses were expensive and needed a lot of people and planning to construct. Tara considered cheap houses that can be build with little effort and local materials an important survival tool. Although, among the elites in big cities, mud construction had become popular because of the breathable and aesthetic walls. However, it was mainly done with rammed earth which required advanced technology and a lot of money. Because Charmadi was remote, that technology was not available there.

But yes, Tara got a ceramic tiled roof which kept the house cool and permeable, all year long. The house was really small but too beautiful to be treated as temporary. Tara was a fan of the tiny house movement and she had read up enough on optimizing space. A small house was also great to practice minimalism because there simply was no place for anything extra. This makeshift house was providing an opportunity to fulfill her long term desire of practicing minimalism while living in a tiny house. All plans to build another house was shelved away for good. Charmadi was teaching her to be content with little. Less was manageable.

Voltaire suggests in his book, Candide, that everyone must cultivate a garden to find real lasting peace. Like the character in Voltaire's story, after chasing all the big goals in life, Tara was happy to settle down and nurture a farm. The Charmadi farm produced the sweetest of bananas, mangoes, and jackfruits. Every three months, Tara sold hundreds of coconuts at the local market. And there was this implicit promise that the land will never let Tara go hungry. There will always be some kind of food, either cultivated or wild. She felt more secure than ever. Neither money nor education had made her feel this secure, in a long time. Tara understood why Indians considered the land their mother. It made her feel secure like she felt in her mother's arms when she was a child.

At first, Tara always sought companions while staying over in Charmadi. She was afraid to stay in a farm alone. But then since good company was not always readily available, Tara decided to overcome her fear of living alone. The Kolumbe village was well populated but it was near a dense forest. Spiders as big as Tara's face would be hiding in all corners of her house. Lizards and centipedes would show up from time to time. If she saw a spider at night, Tara would not sleep till morning. But slowly all her fears vanished when she realized that the insects were more afraid of her than she was of them. Moreover, the spiders, she found out were Rain spiders, and were not very poisonous. Even their stings were not supposed to be too painful. Though the spiders never harmed her. They were smart and reminded Tara of octopuses. They would hide and watch the human of the house. There was this unspoken understanding between Tara and the insects. As soon as she came to stay all the resident insects would vanish from her visibility the very next day. They tried not to bother Tara as much as possible.

There were gaps between the ceramic tiled roof and walls of Tara's house. Bats would enter through these openings and occupy the house, in her absence. At first, Chinnamma chased the bats away with a broom. In the process, she hurt a couple of bats and it was obvious they did not survive. After that Tara shooed the bats away herself making sure no one was hurt. Tara tried not to kill. It was the jungle and the animals did not know they were doing anything wrong in finding shelter in Tara's house. The bats knew that they were annoying Tara and tried to get out as fast as they could. But they panicked and they were disoriented in the day time. Tara had to be patient with them till they found their exit. Soon, Tara sealed all the openings and closed entry for bats for good. Bats were a health hazard and not welcome. Tara did make her peace with insects, though. Not everything required getting used to, because there was plenty to celebrate in Charmadi. Peacocks, kingfishers, and Woodpeckers roamed in her farm. Birdwing is considered the largest butterfly in India and is as large as a tiny bird. Birdwings along with many other exotic butterflies flew all around her tiny house.

There are four stages of a human life in the Varnashrama system in India. The first stage is the Brahmacharya ashrama which is the life of a student. The second is the Grihasta ashrama where you lived the life of a householder. The third stage is the Vanaprastha ashrama which means, literally, the way of the forest. Life in the forest is supposed to prepare you for the fourth and final stage of the Sanyasa ashrama, wherein you lived a life of renunciation. In Charmadi, Tara understood why the Vanaprastha ashrama was so important. The forest teaches you to slow down and observe. Alertness is necessary for survival in the jungle. Before she came to

Charmadi, Tara had little time to watch spiders so closely. If she saw one, she would scream for help and someone would come and kill it. Now she realized that spiders were intelligent and they could communicate with her. These communications were subtle like the weather. You had to become sensitive enough to notice.

In the Indian jungles, for thousands of years, people lived in peace with nature, among snakes, tigers, and other wild animals. But the rules of survival in the forest were definitely different from life outside of it. Tara understood that these rules were based on a profound respect for all living beings. Respect mitigates fear. Courage was necessary to develop skills for survival. In modern times, man is the most feared animal on earth. Everything hides on his arrival. However, in ancient India, an old couple, living in Vanaprastha ashrama, blended well with their environment. They cut all ties with their wealth and family. They chose a lifestyle of minimalism, peace, and the forest, as the days of their lives became numbered. Tara saw glimpses of what life would be like in the Vanaprastha ashrama at Charmadi.

"Jai Jawan, Jai Kisan" was a salutation framed by the Second Prime minister of India, Lal Bahadur shastri. He recognized that the farmer and the soldier were the two most important components of a country. Food security was as important as border security, if not more. Tara had seen countries that depended on other countries for basic necessities like food and medicine brought down on their knees quickly by merchandise sanctions, alone. Another quality a farmer had in common with a soldier is that, he would work hard in all weather. Tara was touched to see her farmer friends, hard at work, in scorching heat and pouring rain.

Farming like soldiering cannot be done for profit. It was duty and not a job. Tara's ancestors grew crops according to soil conditions. They grew multiple crops whose main purpose was to provide food for the family. Only the excess would get sold in markets. They did the important job of feeding a nation. But now Tara saw farmers growing only cash crops. If rubber was profitable one year, all trees would be cut down to grow rubber. In Charmadi, all paddy farms were slowly getting converted in to profitable betelnut plantations. Chasing money in agriculture was futile. What was profitable one year would end up in loss in another. Tara ignored suggestions of growing betelnut trees in her farm. She grew black pepper, coconut trees, cashew nut trees and all kinds of fruit trees, instead. She practiced organic farming, whenever possible. She used solar energy for all her electric needs. She lived a wholesome life, sticking to her belief that money was not the only wealth life provides. The climate of India was fertile. Everything grew here from timber to pepper. There was no need to be greedy. The earth was very generous.

Most people who worked on her farm were people Tara knew from before because of her parents. Sanoj was her cousin who had lived with her parents in his formative years. He had grown in to an expert in all kinds rural farm management related to buying, designing, and running a farm. Others like Baby Chaketh had worked for her parents. Baby Chaketh was skilled at all kinds of farm jobs and was a quick learner. He could cut grass, build houses, plant trees, climb trees, and also cook food. There was nothing he could not do. He knew everyone and went everywhere. Nothing in the village from marriages to funerals happened without the participation of Baby Chaketh.

Tara owed it to her parents for getting the best of help to attend to her farm. It was the affection the farmers felt for Tara's parents that overflowed to her. As they aged, the memory power of her parents diminished. Yet, they remembered minute details of every person they met. They knew their family names and places of origin. They knew the names of their children. Tara's parents really loved people. Cooking for farm help was an ancient tradition in India. Tara's parents always cooked elaborate meals for their farm help. But in modern times, they were buying food from restaurants. No one had the time to cook even for themselves. Slowly, Tara followed tradition and learned to cook for her farm help. She learned to make the parboiled rice they ate and the curries they preferred. That way she felt she was contributing to all the hard work that was going on in her farm. Tara was happy to cook food for her farmer friends knowing that she was helping in a small way towards their good health. The farmers also appreciated the warm home cooked meals and overlooked any errors Tara made.

As soon as the drinking water well had become functional and the house had become barely livable, Jaya visited Charmadi. Jaya performed an elaborate fire ritual called the Agnihotram to purify the space. She then planted a Tulsi plant in front of the house. During Jaya's stay at Charmadi, Tara and Jaya went for long walks every morning and evening. They mediated every day sitting down on the porch floor. They cooked healthy delicious meals which were eaten hot served on banana leaves. Their daily rituals at Charmadi were similar to the ones on their spiritual trips. Somehow Charmadi was more than a farm to them. It promised spiritual progress.

As soon as the Corona restrictions were lifted, the first trip Tara took was to visit Jaya in Trichy. In the Trichy district, the Cauvery river splits into two branches. The northern branch is called Kollidam, and the southern branch is Cauvery. After flowing for about Sixteen Kilometers, the two branches join again, briefly, to form the Srirangam Island. Considering the fact that Cauvery was one of the seven holy rivers of India, Srirangam was, indeed, a blessed island. And Jaya had build a home in Srirangam and was excited to show Tara her setup.

Srirangam housed the Sriranganatha swamy temple which was an ancient Vishnu temple. Srirangam reminded Tara of Badrinath, may be because of the Vishnu temple. Or perhaps, the visit represented abundance that came after the austere pandemic days. Every day hundreds of people visited this temple and it was festive all the time. All around Trichy was history and tradition. At the Tanjavur big temple, Tara and Jaya saw one of the biggest Shiva Lingams in India. They visited the Vekaliyamman temple, Nachiyar kovil, and the Panchavarna Swamy temple in Woraiyur. They also visited the Kattu and Atru Narasimha perumal temples in Trichy, when Jaya's parents also accompanied them. They learned about the Chola kings who build these magnificent temples. Tara and Jaya were having a great time visiting ancient temples, eating delicious food, and wearing fragrant jasmine flowers on their hair, every day.

At Srirangam, the river Cauvery was in her full glory. She would soon branch out to meet the sea a little further within the Tamilnadu state. It was amazing to see how the river who began as a small pond at Talacauvery near Mangalore had become as grand as an ocean at Trichy. The two friends were happy to pay their respects to the River Cauvery and take their holy dips.

Tara also got to spend time with Jaya's parents in this visit and it felt like life had come to a full circle. As a child, Tara visited Jaya's home often. Now she was meeting Jaya's parents as an adult at Srirangam. A little like the River Cauvery. Everyone had changed with time but the love remained. They all enjoyed each other's company immensely. Tara was sad to say goodbye. It was a visit Tara would cherish forever. A life well lived is measured by the memories we make and the memories we take.

CHAPTER 22

Karma Yoga

The ultimate goal of every religion is to attain liberation from death and suffering. Such a spiritual Liberation has many names, and some of them are Moksha, Salvation, Nirvana, Mukti, and Enlightenment. Bhagavad Gita is known as the Moksha sastra, that is, the science of Moksha, and Moksha is clearly defined in the Gita. But the concepts in the Gita do not make sense until you have the right questions. Even the Bhagavad Gita, which literally means the song of God, is a set of answers by Lord Krishna to questions asked by his friend Arjuna, on a battlefield.

Jai's Bhagavad Gita classes were god send for Tara, who was trying to understand Moksha. It took almost two years to complete the first round of reading the Bhagavad Gita. The concepts in the Gita were complex and new for Tara. Jai did a great job of answering her many questions, and his Bhagavad Gita reading course became the closure of the spiritual journey, Tara began after her Art of living course. Tara could, finally, summarize her understanding of Moksha, with the aid of the Bhagavad Gita. In her summary, Tara decided to use Lord Krishna's words, wherever possible, to remain close to the intended meaning. When Tara first started reading the Gita, she had misinterpreted the content many times. The topics in the Gita were unlike anything she had heard before, and it took a while for Tara, to suspend her own intellect, and simply listen.

Who were the people who sought Moksha? In India, it is believed that the purpose of a human birth is to attain Moksha. In ancient times, in the last stage of life, that is, in the Sanyasa Ashrama, retired people dedicated all their time seeking Moksha. People, who have a spiritual disposition and choose religion as a career, also make Moksha their end goal. However, the most common cause for seeking Moksha is overwhelming grief. Disappointment, in the world we live in, triggers a search for the meaning of life. In fact, the Bhagavad Gita came about as an antidote for Arjuna's deep sorrow. Arjuna who faces a battle that will result in the death of many of his teachers, friends, and family, says in Verse 2.8,

"I do not see anything that will remove the sorrow that dries up my senses, even if I were to obtain an unrivaled and prosperous kingdom on earth and sovereignty over the denizens of heaven."

In Verse 1.46, Arjuna says,

"It would be better if, with weapons in hand, the sons of Dhritarashtra kill me unarmed and unresisting on the battlefield."

Thus, Arjuna who was an accomplished warrior and the beloved of the masses, was now in such a state of despair, that he did not even care about being alive. Addressing Arjuna's grief, in Verse 2.11, Lord Krishna says with a smile,

"You are mourning for that which is not worthy of grief. The wise lament neither for the living nor for the dead."

Tara had come to terms, for a while now that, there was no end to suffering. There was only learning to cope with suffering in a civilized way. Neither does time heal pain. It only inflicts bigger pains to make the past pain look easier.

Some religions promised lasting happiness after death. However, Lord Krishna says, in the Gita, that there can be no grief for a wise person, who knows the truth about oneself. In Verse 2.20, Lord Krishna says,

"This self is never born, nor does it die. It is not that, having been, it ceases to exist again. This self is unborn, eternal, undergoes no change whatsoever, and is ever new. When the body is destroyed, it is not destroyed."

Tara reckoned that the self, mentioned by Lord Krishna, was the soul, Tara had heard about from her Christian upbringing. She had learned that the soul would survive the death of the body. She never had dwelled on the birth of the soul. Though we celebrate birthdays as the day, when the child came out of the mother's womb, the child was alive months before that. Moreover, according to the Gita, the soul of the child always existed. It is unborn and cannot die. However, it was futile for Tara to look for a quick description of the soul because in Verse 2.25, Lord Krishna says,

"This self is said to be unmanifest, not an object of thought, and not subject to change."

It was a real dilemma that Tara could neither see the soul nor know the soul. It was told in the Gita, that to receive this knowledge, the mind had to be prepared. Equanimity was the primary goal of Vipassana meditation. In the Gita, also, equanimity was an important prerequisite for attaining Moksha, as Lord Krishna says in Verse 2.15,

"That person who is not affected by happiness and distress, and remains steady in both, becomes eligible for liberation."

Anicca, the impermanence of a state, addressed so frequently in the Vipassana course by Goenkaji, was also pointed out in Verse 2.14, by Lord Krishna,

"The contacts of the sense organs with the sensory world which give rise to cold and heat, pleasure and pain, which have the nature of coming and going, are not constant. Endure them."

In Verse 2.64, Lord Krishna says,

"One whose mind is controlled, moving in the world of objects with the sense organs under his or her control, free from likes and dislikes, attains tranquility."

After every Vipassana course, by getting rid of a lot of likes and dislikes, Tara always felt an intense peace. Tara was pleased to see the many similarities in Vipassana techniques and the instructions in the Bhagavad Gita.

In Verse 2.65, Lord Krishna emphasizes tranquility to gain knowledge,

"When the mind is tranquil, destruction of all pain and sorrow happens because the knowledge of one who is tranquil minded soon becomes well established."

In Verse 2.66, Lord Krishna says,

"For the one who is not tranquil, there is no knowledge. For the one who is not tranquil, there is no contemplation and for the one who is not contemplative, there is no peace. For the one who has no peace, how can there be happiness?"

Lord Krishna prescribes Karma Yoga, which means performing actions without being attached to the fruits of action, as a path to gain equanimity.

In Verse 2.40, Lord Krishna praises Karma Yoga,

"In this, there is no waste of effort, nor are the opposite results produced. Even very little of this Karma Yoga protects one from great fear."

In Verse 2.47, Lord Krishna says,

"Your choice is in action only, never in the results thereof. Do not be the author of the results of action. Let your attachment not be to inaction."

In Verse 2.48, Lord Krishna says,

"Be steadfast in the performance of your duty, abandoning attachment to success and failure. Such equanimity is called Yoga."

Work was pleasure for Tara, but whenever she did not get the desired results, she became unhappy. It felt as though all her efforts were in vain. In Verse 5.12, Lord Krishna says,

"The one who is endowed with Karma Yoga, giving up the result of action, gains a composure born of a commitment to a life of Karma yoga. Whereas one who is not committed to a life of karma yoga, led by desire, is bound, being attached to the result of action."

Desires are the root cause of misery as Lord Krishna says, in Verse 3.41,

"Bring the senses under control and slay this enemy called desire, which is the embodiment of sin and destroys knowledge and realization."

In Verse 2.62, Lord Krishna says,

"In the person who dwells upon objects, an attachment is born with reference to them. From attachment is born desire and from desire, anger is born."

In Verse 2.63, Lord Krishna says,

"From anger comes delusion and from delusion comes the loss of memory. Because of the loss of memory, the mind becomes incapacitated and when the mind is incapacitated, the person is destroyed."

After gaining equanimity, a seeker could choose the path of Karma Sanyasa, which means, renunciation of all duties and contemplate only on God and soul. Lord Krishna says in Verse 6.3,

"To the person who is aspiring for perfection in Yoga, Karma Yoga is said to be the means, to the person who is already elevated in Yoga, Karma Sanyasa is said to be the means."

However, in Verse 6.2, Lord Krishna says,

"Sanyasa is nondifferent from Yoga, for none can become enlightened without renouncing worldly desires."

An enlightened person is free of all responsibilities, as Krishna say in Verse 3.18,

"Selfrealized souls have nothing to gain or lose either in discharging or renouncing their duties. Nor do they need to depend on other living beings to fulfill their selfinterest."

In Verse 2.52, Lord Krishna says,

"When your intellect crosses over the impurity of delusion, then you shall gain a dispassion towards what has been heard and what is yet to be heard."

This dispassion was very important, as Tara would find out, because to accept the concepts in the Gita, a lot of her old notions had to go. Letting go was not an easy process. In the Verses 13.7 to 13.11, Lord Krishna provides a long list of qualities, a person requires, to let go of all obstacles to the path of wisdom,

"Absence of conceit, absence of pretension, nonviolence, accommodation, straightforwardness, service to the teacher, cleanliness of body and mind, steadfastness, mastery over the mind, dispassion toward the objects of the senses, absence of pride, seeing clearly the defects of pain in birth, death, old age, and disease, absence of a sense of ownership, absence of obsession towards son, spouse, home, and the like, always evenness of mind regarding the gain of the desired and undesired, an unswerving exclusive devotion to God, an inclination for solitary places, no longing for the company of people, always dwelling upon the knowledge centered on the self, keeping in view the purpose of the knowledge of the truth, all this that was told is the means to knowledge, and what is opposite to this is ignorance."

CHAPTER 23

Brahma Vidya

In the Gita, Lord Krishna presents himself as Ishwara, God, and is always addressed as Sri Bhagawan. In her summary of Brahma Vidya, Tara reminded herself, to do the same.

The entire teaching in the Gita could be condensed in to the equation "Tat tvam asi" which literally means "That thou art." Here, Tat is Ishwara, and the meaning of the word, Tvam, is you. To understand this radical statement, the concepts of Sat and Asat had to be understood first. Asat, also known as Mithya, means something that does not exist independently. Because asat has no independent existence, it is not separate from that upon which it depends. For example, a pot made of clay, is also clay. Sat, on the other hand, is what exists independent of anything else, that is pure existence. Sat is that, which never changes, it has no nonexistence. Observe that, there is no selfexistent thing among all the objects of the world. A pot, for example, is made of clay. The clay can be broken down, further to atoms, which can be further broken down, till nothing remains, except sat. Because sat has no nonexistence.

Sri Bhagawan begins his teaching of Brahma Vidya with the Verse 13.1,

"This body is termed as the field, and the one who knows this body, is the knower of the field, by people who discern the truth about both."

In Verses 13.5 and 13.6, Sri Bhagawan says,

"The five great elements, the ego, the intellect, the unmanifest cause of everything, the ten senses, the mind, and the five objects of the senses, desire and aversion, happiness and misery, the body, cognition, fortitude – all these comprise the field and its modifications."

The five great elements are the earth, water, fire, air, and space. The five knowledge-acquiring senses are the ears, the eyes, nose, tongue, and the sense of touch. The five working senses are the organ of speech, the hands, the feet, the organ of excretion, and the organ of reproduction. The five objects of the senses are smell, taste, warmth, touch, and sound. The field, also known as prakriti, constitutes the material cause in the creation of everything in the universe. Everything in prakriti is asat. It is important to note that the body and mind are also asat.

In Verse 13.26, Sri Bhagawan says,

"Whatever moving or unmoving being you see in existence, know it is born because of the connection between the field and the knower of the field."

Ishwara is the knower of the field as Sri Bhagawan says, in Verse 13.2,

"May you know me as the knower of the body in all the bodies. That knowledge of the body and the knower of the body, is truly the knowledge."

That knowledge of the body and the knower of the body, which grants Moksha, is the knowledge of Brahman, as Sri Bhagawan says, in Verse 13.12,

"I shall now reveal to you that which ought to be known, and by knowing which, one attains immortality. That is said to be Brahman, which has no beginning, is limitless, and is neither existent nor non-existent."

Brahman is pure consciousness, that illumine both knowledge and ignorance. It allows everything to exist including darkness, as Sri Bhagawan says, in Verse 13.17,

"Brahman is the source of light in all luminaries, and is said to be beyond ignorance. He is knowledge, the object of knowledge, and the goal of knowledge. He is present in the minds of all living beings."

Thus, Brahman is sat-chit-ananda, which means, existence, consciousness, and limitlessness.

Even though, Brahman does not exist as one of the objects of creation, all objects of creation reveal how he is not non-existent. In Verse 13.13, Sri Bhagawan says,

"Everywhere are his hands and feet, eyes, heads, and faces. His ears too are in all places, for he pervades everything in the universe."

In Verse 13.16, Sri Bhagawan says,

"He is indivisible, yet he appears to be divided amongst living beings. He is the sustainer, annihilator, and creator of all beings and elements."

Finally, in Verse 13.22, Sri Bhagawan reveals "Tat tvam asi",

"The witness, permitter, sustainer, enjoyer, limitless creator, also called the limitless self, is the self, who is limitless in this body."

In Verse 13.15, Sri Bhagawan says,

"Brahman exists outside and inside all living beings, those that are moving and not moving. He is subtle, and hence, he is incomprehensible. He is very far, but he is also very near."

Brahman is near because he is yourself. Brahman is far because, if you do not recognize Brahman as yourself, you will never find him. Because the one who looks for Brahman is Brahman.

Prakriti is the material cause of creation, as Sri Bhagawan says, in Verse 13.20,

"Prakriti is said to be the cause in the creation of the physical body and the instruments, the self is said to be the cause with reference to the state of being the experiencer of pleasure and pain."

The three gunas (qualities) of Prakriti are satva – purity and knowledge, rajas – activity and passion, tamas – ignorance, inertia, and laziness.

In Verse 13.19, Sri Bhagawan says,

"Know that prakriti and the self are both beginningless. Also know that the modifications and qualities are indeed born of prakriti."

In Verse 14.5, Sri Bhagawan says,

"Satva, rajas, and tamas, the qualities existing in prakriti, bind the eternal self to the perishable body."

In Verse 13.21, Sri Bhagawan says,

"The self seated in prakriti, enjoys the qualities born of prakriti. His attachment to the gunas becomes the cause for birth in superior and inferior wombs."

The self neither performs any action nor does any action affect it, as Sri Bhagawan says, in Verse 13.31,

"The limitless self is imperishable, without beginning, and without any attributes. Although obtained in the body, it neither perform action, nor is it affected by the results of action."

In Verse 13.29, Sri Bhagawan says,

"He who sees that by prakriti alone actions are being performed in all ways, and who sees the self as a nondoer, he alone sees."

In Verse 13.34, Sri Bhagawan says,

"Those who perceive, with the eyes of knowledge, the difference between the body and the knower of the body, and the process of release from prakriti, attain the supreme destination."

In Verse 13.30, Sri Bhagawan describes a person who knows the truth of Brahman,

"When one sees clearly, the condition of distinction in the beings, as having its existence in one self, and from that alone is its distinctions, then he gains the realization of the Brahman."

For Tara, the most pertinent verse in all of Bhagavad Gita, remained the Verse 2.16, in which Sri Bhagawan says,

"For the asat, there is never any being. For the sat, there is never any non-being. The ultimate truth of both of these is seen by the knowers of the truth."

Tara knew her own life was like writing on the wind. Every moment passed never to return. Some moments were retained, a bit longer, only in the memory. Her life was asat. Only thing that remained, waking, sleeping, or dreaming was Brahman – pure consciousness and existence. The difference between her and Ishwara was only asat, for which, there never was any being. She could finally, tell herself, "Tat tvam asi."

CHAPTER 24

Moksha

Moksha is considered to be freedom from death and suffering. In the Gita, moksha is attained by gaining Brahma Vidya. Applying Brahma Vidya, when you understand nothing affects the self, suffering, even death, becomes vacuous.

In Verse 13.32, Lord Krishna says,

"Just as the all pervasive space, because it is subtle, is not affected, so too the self, abiding, in all states in the body, is not affected."

In Verse 2.30, Lord Krishna tells Arjuna not to grieve the death of his loved ones,

"This self, the indweller of the bodies of all beings, is ever indestructible. Therefore, you ought not to grieve for all these people."

Lord Krishna tells Arjuna that, even if he decides to reject Brahma Vidya, he should not grieve. In Verse 2.26, Lord Krishna says,

"And if you take the self to have constant birth and death, even then, you ought not to grieve for the self in this manner."

In Verse 2.28, Lord Krishna says,

"All beings are unmanifest in the beginning, manifest in the middle, and again unmanifest in the end. What indeed is there to grieve about?"

Thus, understanding the nature of asat, it was futile to grieve. If a mad dog bites you, you do not grieve. You understand the nature of the mad dog and do what is to be done. Do your karma yoga to deal with asat. The universe is like a turbulent ocean which is only peaceful at times. The only thing in our control, is to steady the boat we are in. That is, control our likes and dislikes, and attain tranquility to gain freedom from suffering.

Apart from freedom from death and suffering, Moksha is also considered as freedom from the cycle of death and rebirth. Applying Brahma Vidya, one can address this as "If I am not born, there is no question of being reborn." Tara had never been interested in the concept of rebirth. Her entire focus was on making the life, she was living, as pleasant as possible. The only way, she knew, she could affect someone after her death, was through genetics. The concept of rebirth, made Tara think about the role, genetics played in the life of a person. It was a project she would consider working on in the future.

Tara had always associated Moksha with accomplishing infinite compassion. This also was established as true because, after attaining Moksha, when you have attained tranquility and freedom from asat, what remains would be only compassion. When the hate is removed, all that remains is love. Love, you realize, is your essential nature. Just like, when you remove the entire material universe from your mind, you will not meet with emptiness. Instead, you will meet with the fullness of Brahman.

Attaining Moksha also meant answering the question "Who is God?." In Verses 7.4 and 7.5, Lord Krishna says,

"Earth, water, fire, air, space, mind, intellect and indeed the sense of doership – thus this prakriti of mine is divided in an eight-fold way. This is my lower nature. Whereas, please understand the one other than this, my higher nature, is the essential nature of the individual, by which this world is sustained."

In Verse 7.6, Lord Krishna says,

"Please understand that all beings and elements have their cause in this twofold nature. Therefore, I am the one from whom this entire world comes, so too, I am the one into whom everything resolves."

In Verse 13.27, Lord Krishna says,

"The one who sees Ishwara, as remaining the same in all beings, as the one who is imperishable in the things that are perishing, is the one who truly sees."

In Swami Dayananda Saraswati's words,

"We do not say there are many gods. We do not say there is one God. We say there is only God."

Lord Krishna says faith is beneficial, even if a person did not have any knowledge of Brahma Vidya. Ishwara blesses the faithful by granting wishes. In Verse 9.23, Lord Krishna says,

"Even those devotees who faithfully worship other gods also worship only me. But they do so backed by ignorance."

In Verse 7.21 Lord Krishna says,

"Whoever be the devotee and in whichever form, he wishes to worship with faith, indeed that same faith, I make firm for him."

In Verse 7.22 Lord Krishna says,

"Endowed with faith, the devotee worships a particular celestial god and obtains the objects of desire. But in reality, I alone arrange these benefits."

Tara had experienced the prayer-answering and wish granting God, many times in her life. Tara realized that most of her wishes, came from the universe, and it was not surprising that, they fructified. The more tranquil you were, the more in tune you were, to the wishes of the universe. This was the very reason the prayers of saints and other holy people, were answered more faster and more frequently, than regular people.

Ishwara also protects righteousness on earth as Lord Krishna says, in Verse 4.7,

"Whenever there is a decline in righteousness and an increase in unrighteousness, at that time I manifest myself on earth."

In Verse 4.8, Lord Krishna says,

"To protect the righteous, to annihilate the wicked, and to reestablish the principles of dharma, I appear on this earth, age after age."

That Ishwara, himself, comes to help, is the basis of hope for humankind. Ishwara came to earth, as Lord Krishna to help in the Mahabharat war, and destroy the Kauravas. It was necessary for the Kauravas to go, for the Pandavas to come. The Kauravas had become very corrupt and even tried to disrobe Princess Draupadi in public, in a courtroom, in front of elders. All those who watched silently, had to go, for righteousness to prevail.

Similarly, Jesus Christ was born on earth to bring in sweeping changes. A society, that could legally, make an injured man carry a heavy cross, and then nail him to that same cross, to torture him to death, was vile beyond doubt. It had to go.

Messiahs and avatars brought in sweeping changes. Even otherwise, the universe, inherently, has a strong inclination towards righteousness. Which is why people like Hitler had to go. Life has a strong instinct for survival of the species. Righteousness was in the interest of survival. History was witness to how good and peaceful regimes lasted much longer than the evil ones.

The inevitable question facing Tara was, "Did she attain Moksha?" To her aid, came Arjuna's question to Lord Krishna in Verse 2.54,

"What is the description of a person of firm wisdom, one whose mind abides in the self? How does such a person, whose mind is not shaken by anything, speak, sit, and walk?"

In verse 2.55, Lord Krishna says,

"When a person gives up all the desires, as they appear in the mind, happy in oneself, with oneself alone, that person is said to be one of ascertained knowledge."

In Verse 2.56, Lord Krishna says,

"The one who is not affected by adversities, who is without yearning for pleasures, and is free from longing, fear, and anger is said to be a wise person whose knowledge remains."

In Verse 2.57, Lord Krishna says,

"For the one who is unattached in all situations, who neither rejoices on gaining the pleasant, nor hates the unpleasant, his knowledge is well established."

Tara could not say, honestly that, she was not affected by adversities. She was affected, especially, when her loved ones suffered. But she could regain composure more quickly, now. Moreover, the attachments she had now, were bound to diminish as life progressed, because death and distance were always at play. An attitude of Karmayoga and regular practice of Vipassana meditation helped her maintain her tranquility. Surprisingly, after all the effort, Tara was not too concerned about attaining Moksha. Tara was in the moment, cherishing her loved ones, enjoying the abundance presented to her, by life. In India, Lord Krishna stood for infinite joy. Tara began to experience some of that joy. In the journey of understanding God, she had ended up understanding herself, and the miracle of life.

Somewhere, sometime, many moons ago, Tara had asked the question "why?." That question, she realized, was not tenable and will never be answered.